TAKEN

TAKEN

NORAH McCLINTOCK

ORCA BOOK PUBLISHERS

Library and Archives Canada Cataloguing in Publication

McClintock, Norah
Taken / Norah McClintock.

ISBN 978-1-55469-152-4

I. Title.

PS8575.C62T35 2009   jC813'.54   C2009-902065-3

First published in the United States, 2009
Library of Congress Control Number: 2009925695

Summary: When Stephanie is abducted and left alone in the woods, it takes all of her strength to survive.

Orca Book Publishers gratefully acknowledges the support for its publishing programs provided by the following agencies: the Government of Canada through the Book Publishing Industry Development Program and the Canada Council for the Arts, and the Province of British Columbia through the BC Arts Council and the Book Publishing Tax Credit.

Design by Teresa Bubela
Cover photo by Larry Lilac, GetStock.com

ORCA BOOK PUBLISHERS
PO Box 5626, STN. B
VICTORIA, BC CANADA
V8R 6S4

ORCA BOOK PUBLISHERS
PO Box 468
CUSTER, WA USA
98240-0468

www.orcabook.com
Printed and bound in Canada.
Printed on 100% PCW recycled paper.

12 11 10 09 • 4 3 2 1

To Andrew Wooldridge: I think he knows why.

ONE

M y stomach clenched as the bus rumbled across the county line. In less than ten minutes it would pull into the parking lot at Ralph's, and I would have to get off. I wished it would never get there. Allison wished exactly the opposite.

"I can't wait to get home," she said. "I can't wait to show my mom what I bought."

Allison was my best friend. We'd met in fourth grade after my dad had been hired as a manager at a nuclear power plant and we had moved from the city, where I had been born, to a small town about twenty miles from the plant. Allison had lived in the town her whole life. Her dad was a pharmacist. He owned a drugstore on the main street. Her mom was a hairdresser. She had her own salon. Allison and I hit it off right away. She made me forget how much I missed my friends back home. It wasn't long before we were doing everything together. Today we had taken the bus into the city and spent the whole day shopping.

"Steph?" Allison touched my arm. "Steph, what's the matter? I thought we had a great time, but you haven't said a word for the past half hour."

Reluctantly I pulled my eyes away from the bus window.

"Is it Gregg?" Allison said.

I nodded. "He's such a dick."

"Maybe they'll break up."

"I wish."

Boy, did I wish! I didn't even know what my mom saw in him. He was nothing at all like my dad. My dad had a couple of university degrees and traveled all over the world before he met my mom and got married. He read all the time. He was smarter than almost anyone else I'd ever met, but he never showed off. He also cared about important things—things besides making money. He liked to spend his time helping people and volunteering in the community. He was involved in a couple of service clubs and some local charities. Everyone liked him. Everyone said what a nice guy he was.

Gregg, on the other hand, had barely made it through high school. He worked at a car-parts factory that had gone down to half-shifts months ago. He was trying to make up for his reduced wages by working for a buddy of his who had a vending-machine operation. A couple of days every two weeks, Gregg drove all over the area, filling machines and collecting money. His idea of a good time was playing poker or going snowmobiling with a bunch of his loser friends he'd known since high school. His big dream was being his own boss in his own business (I never was clear on just what kind of business he had in mind or was even qualified to run) and making a pile of money that he could spend on a new boat, a new car every year and—this was the one he made the biggest deal about—an outdoor hot tub so that he and my mom could sit outside under the stars, drinking champagne and fooling around. Yuck!

Unlike my dad, Gregg had never been anywhere. Worse, he was actually proud that he'd been born and raised, and had spent his whole life so far, in the same stifling little town. I'd lost count of the number of times I'd heard him say that he would never live within a hundred miles of a city. He said cities were filled with concrete and smog and people living on top of each other, like ants in an anthill. He said if you looked at the crime rates, you'd see that most of the people who got murdered were city people. What an idiot. First of all, didn't he know that something like eighty percent of the people in the whole country lived in cities, so of course it stood to reason that most of the people who got murdered got murdered in cities? And second, it wasn't like there was no crime at all out in the country. For the past two months, everyone in every small town up here had been freaking out because of the two girls who had disappeared. One day they were there, the next they were gone.

When the first girl vanished, the police said they believed she had either run away or got lost. They thought this because she was a city girl who had moved out to the country less than a year ago and her parents said that she hadn't settled in yet. Her mom was afraid she might have tried to hitchhike back to the city. Her father had another idea. He said she'd started taking walks in the woods behind the subdivision where they lived. The woods were thicker than they looked from the subdivision, and they went on for a long way. He thought she was in there, either hiding because she was mad at her parents or lost because she had no sense of direction. The police mounted an all-out search for her. Dozens of volunteers helped them, combing the woods, the fields around the woods and the countryside beyond that. They looked for six days before they called it off. They said they had exhausted all the possibilities.

Two weeks after they stopped looking, a man out walking with his dog found her—*not alive*, as my mom put it. It turned out she had been murdered and then buried out in the scrub behind an abandoned sugar shack. Whoever had buried her hadn't dug a deep grave. Because of that, an animal got at her, which is how the man and his dog found her. The dog started barking, and when the man went over to see what was wrong, he saw a hand lying on the ground. That's it, just a hand. The man called the police and they brought in their own dog, and that dog led the cops to the rest of her. It was on the news for days. Everybody talked about it—especially because two days before that, the second girl had disappeared.

At first the police said that there was no evidence to suggest that the second girl's disappearance had anything to do with what had happened to the first girl. At least, that's what they said publicly. Nobody believed that was what they really thought.

"Two girls, both the same age, both with long dark hair—of course they're related," Derek Fowler, who was in three of my classes, said. "And look at the circumstances—they were both supposedly on their way home, both just after dark, but neither one ever got there. Trust me, there's a serial killer out there." Derek claimed to know everything there was to know about serial killers. He considered himself an expert. "If the first girl turned up dead, you can bet your life the same thing will happen to the second girl. Serial killers are all about patterns and rituals. If they ever get caught, that's how the police get them—by studying their patterns and rituals. The FBI has a whole training program on serial killers." Derek talked a lot about joining the FBI one day and learning to track serial killers. Most of the time, he sounded like he might turn out to be a serial killer himself. But not this time. Almost everyone in town was thinking the same thing Derek was.

Derek claimed that the police were thinking it too, even if they never came right out and said so. "Either that or they're totally incompetent," Derek said.

There were just too many coincidences for the two disappearances to be completely unrelated.

The thought that there was a serial killer out there put people on edge. Parents warned their daughters never to go anywhere alone. They told them never to talk to strangers. They wagged their fingers and said they should never get into anyone's car, not even someone they might have seen around and who looked friendly, because, they said, you never know. We had a special assembly at school where a cop told us more or less the same thing. The school sent a special newsletter out to parents with a checklist to go over with their kids—what to do and what not to do. My mom made me read it out loud to her so that she knew that I knew what was in it. When I finished, she said, "Do what they say, Stephanie." She also said, "Don't even think about running away again. What happened to those two girls could happen to you." Just to make sure I didn't forget, she stuck an article from the local newspaper to the fridge door. It outlined the details of both disappearances and had pictures of both the girls on it.

"Hey, those girls look just like you," Gregg said one morning when I went downstairs for breakfast. He was standing in front of the fridge with a carton of orange juice in his hand, and I could tell by the dribble of juice on his chin that he'd been drinking straight from it.

"Mom told you not to do that," I said.

"Mom told you not to do that," he repeated in a high-pitched voice, doing an imitation of me that made me sound like a bitchy little princess, which I'm not.

"Well, she did," I said. God, he was so annoying. "It's disgusting."

"It's how I do things."

"Yeah? Well, if you want to do disgusting things like that, you should buy your own juice instead of always mooching off us." I never touched any container of juice or milk that was open in the fridge. I didn't want his germs.

Gregg gave me a sharp look. I thought he was going to say something else, but my mom came into the kitchen and all of a sudden he was all smiles. He was always all smiles around her.

"What's going on?" my mom said after she kissed him on the lips, which was even more revolting than watching Gregg drinking orange juice straight from the carton.

"I was just telling Steph to be careful," Gregg said. "You know, because there's a killer on the loose."

He made spooky ghost noises, like that was going to scare me.

"It's not funny, Gregg," my mom said. "I wish the police would catch the guy. Then we could all stop worrying."

I hadn't even started worrying, mainly because neither of the two girls who had disappeared lived in our town. The first one lived just outside a hamlet that consisted of four corners (gas station, motel and a few small stores) surrounded by mile after mile of farmland. It was lonely out there, which not only made it a perfect place to grab a girl unnoticed but also explained why the girl hadn't settled in. Living there had probably driven her crazy. The second girl lived down the highway in a beach town that was filled with tourists all summer and was pretty much dead for the rest of the year—another perfect place for someone to grab a girl. But it was different for me. I lived in the biggest town in the county. There were always people on the streets. There were always people watching. Too many people, if you ask me, paying too much attention to everyone else's business. I told my mom she was overreacting.

All too soon, the bus pulled into the parking lot at Ralph's, a combination restaurant and grocery store on Elgin Street that doubled as the intercity bus station. I checked my watch. We had arrived right on schedule. Allison was the second to last person to get off the bus. I was the last person. A big part of me wanted to hide in the back, a stowaway on the return trip to the city. I wished I still had some friends back there that I could stay with, but I had been up here too long.

"I'd get one of my parents to drive you, except they aren't home," Allison said. "But I can call Judd. He won't mind giving you a lift."

Judd was Allison's older brother. Judd and Allison lived three doors down from Ralph's. I lived on the other side of town.

"I'll be fine," I said. "Besides, after sitting on that bus for the last three hours, I need to stretch my legs. I'll walk."

"Are you sure?" Allison said. I nodded. But she wouldn't let it go. "Maybe you should at least phone home first so your mom can look out for you," she said.

"She's not home. She's at her book-club meeting. And Gregg's out on a run." Thank God. I would have the house to myself, which was exactly how I liked it. "I'm going to go home and have a bubble bath." Taking a nice long soak in the tub was one of my favorite things to do.

Allison still didn't look happy. "I'll walk with you," she said. "When we get to your house, I'll call Judd and he can come and get me."

See what I mean about Allison? She was willing to walk all the way across town with me just to make sure that I'd be safe. She was the best friend ever.

"You sound like my mom," I said. "You worry too much. I'll be fine. I'll call you tomorrow. I promise."

I walked down to the end of Elgin Street, turned up Elm Street and made a left on Poplar. I followed Poplar until I came to an open field. It was large and dark and mostly hidden from the view of the houses near it by a border of hedges and mature trees. Before we moved to town, the field had been part of a farm. Then the farmer sold his land to a developer, who built the subdivision where we lived and another subdivision after that. Nothing had been built on this field yet. It had stood empty for as long as I could remember—except for a couple of big For Sale signs. At this time of year, the field consisted mostly of weeds and tall grass. The town mowed it in the summer so it didn't look that bad and so kids could play softball or football. There was a row of trees at one end and some big clumpy bushes dotting it that flowered in spring. There were also a couple of paths cut through the weeds and the grass by all the people who took shortcuts through the field.

For the first time ever, I thought about taking the long way around. But my house was just on the other side. If I cut across the field like I always did, like all the kids on my street did when they went to school or into town, I would be home in less than half the time it would take to go the long way. Besides, I was tired and hungry, and my mom had said she was going to leave supper for me. It seemed like a no-brainer.

Still, I stood for a moment at the edge of the field, scanning it—just to be sure. I didn't see anyone. But one part of my brain said, *Maybe someone is hiding behind a tree or a For Sale sign or in the bushes.* The other part of my brain said, *Get real, Steph, and get home.*

I thought about the first girl who had been taken and who was the only one they had found so far. I wondered exactly what had happened to her. Had a car pulled up alongside her, the driver maybe asking her for directions and then, when she got close enough, grabbing her and dragging her inside with him? Had she been dumb enough to hitch-hike and get into a car with just a guy in it or maybe a couple of guys? Or had she been jumped? Had she been walking home, like I was, thinking about school or her friends or what she was going to do on the weekend, when all of a sudden someone had attacked her or knocked her out or…?

I told myself I was being ridiculous. Just because my mom thought there was some kind of boogeyman out there didn't mean it was true. I mean, seriously, what were the chances?

I started across the field. I admit it, I walked a little faster than usual. I also admit that I couldn't stop glancing back over my shoulder, which was something I didn't ordinarily do. As I walked, I felt a tingle at the back of my neck, like someone was staring at me, but when I turned around, there was no one there. Mom is definitely overreacting, I thought. Worse, her overreacting is contagious.

I was halfway across the field when someone grabbed me from behind.

My instinct was to spin around to see who it was, but an iron-like arm closed around my throat and a steely hand clamped itself over my mouth and nose. I felt cold all over, like the temperature around me had dropped to subarctic levels. I thought, This can't be happening to me. I struggled. I kicked.

I couldn't breathe. The hand over my mouth and nose was cutting off my air supply. My head started to spin. I had to get free before I passed out.

Suddenly the hand let go. I opened my mouth to scream, but the arm around my throat squeezed tighter. I reached behind me to claw at my assailant, desperate to get his arm off me. I tried to scratch his face or his neck or anything else I could reach. Then I felt a jab in my arm. The pain was short and sharp, like a bee sting. I felt numb all over.

My mom always said that some people wake up fast and some people wake up slowly. She said my dad's eyes used to pop open at the first sound of the alarm every morning, and he would immediately leap out of bed, ready to tackle the day. Not me. I always took my time. My mom said I was like that even when I was a baby. She said I would lie in my crib with my eyes closed, but she knew I was awake. She said I was gathering myself. She said she did the same thing. She liked to lie quietly in bed and gradually let the day seep into her bones.

That's what I did when I woke up. I lay in my bed with my eyes closed and let the day seep into my bones.

I thought about my dream. It had been so crazy.
Allison was going to have a good laugh when I told
her about it. She would probably say something like,
"You make fun of everyone for overreacting, but if you
ask me, your subconscious is as worried as everyone
else is." Allison was very big on the subconscious.

I took a deep breath and started to stretch.

That's when I realized something was wrong.

Very wrong.

I couldn't move my arms or legs.

I opened my eyes and peered blearily around.
Instantly I felt sick to my stomach. No, I thought.
No, *no, NO!*

I wasn't on my nice soft mattress between the
crisp sheets on my bed. Instead, I was on the floor,
and the carpet was missing. I tugged on my arms,
but they still wouldn't move. At first I couldn't figure
out what was wrong. My brain wasn't working properly. It felt heavy and wooly. My head ached. I had
trouble focusing, and once I did, I couldn't think
straight enough to absorb my surroundings. It took
a few moments for it to sink in that not only was
I not in my room, I wasn't even in my house. My
heart started to race. All of a sudden I was gasping
in air so fast that I felt faint. I was sure I was going

to pass out. I squeezed my eyes shut—maybe I was in the middle of one of those dreams, you know, the ones where you dream that you wake up but really you're still asleep. I drew in a few breaths and lay quietly until I was sure I was wide awake.

I opened my eyes again, blinked and looked around. An icy feeling spread through my body, just like it had when Clark Adderly, the chief of police, came to our house and spoke to my mom in a soft voice while she sobbed on the sofa. I hadn't wanted to believe what had happened then, just like I didn't want to believe what I was seeing now. That same iciness that I had felt the night before crept into every part of my body, freezing me solid so that I could barely breathe.

I was in some kind of a cabin. It was small and grimy. The wood floor was bare and cold. So were the walls. They hadn't been painted. The only thing on them was a calendar hanging on a nail. It was from a hardware store. The edges were curled. It was ten years out of date.

Whose cabin was this? Where was it? What was I doing here?

And why couldn't I move?

Because I was tied up.

My wrists were bound tightly behind my back. My ankles were tied too and had been pulled back behind me. When I tried to move my legs, the rope around my wrists tightened. I realized that my wrists and ankles had been tied with the same rope, the way you'd tie up an animal so that it wouldn't be able to move. I couldn't stand. I couldn't even sit up.

Thought after thought exploded in my brain, *bang, bang, bang*, like a series of gunshots.

Thought: My mom had been right.

Thought: I hoped she had called the cops. I hoped they were looking for me.

Thought: I hoped she didn't think I ran away again. If she did, she'd have the cops looking in all the wrong places. They wouldn't find me until it was too late—assuming they ever found me.

Thought: Someone grabbed me and brought me here.

Thought: The two girls who disappeared must have felt the same panic that had gripped me and was squeezing me so hard I thought it would crush my heart.

Thought: Whoever took me and brought me to this place must be around here somewhere.

Thought: Maybe he—it's always a he when a girl is missing—was outside right now. Maybe he was reaching out with one hand to push the door open. Maybe he was about to step inside.

Thought: When he did, he was going to do to me what he did to those two girls.

Thought: *I'm going to die.*

THREE

I lay on the gritty wooden floor of the filthy shack, frozen with terror. For weeks I had been hearing about the two girls who had disappeared, but I had never in a million years thought that anything like that would ever happen to me.

But here I was, tied up, groggy, panic-stricken—and waiting. Waiting for whoever had taken me to return. Waiting for whatever had happened to the girl who had been found "not alive" to happen to me. Waiting for whatever had happened to the other girl to happen to me. And the whole time my brain kept screaming, *This can't be real! It just can't be.*

But it was real.

I lay still, holding my breath and listening for any sound of movement outside the shack. But all I could hear was the hammering of my heart in my chest. What if he was on the other side of the door? What if his hand was on the knob and he was about to turn it?

I fought back tears. I told myself that this was no time to cry. It was the time to do something. I don't know what those other girls did when they were taken, but I knew what I was going to do: I was going to fight back. What choice did I have? What did I have to lose?

I forced myself to breathe. Breathe and think.

I listened again—and heard nothing except for the occasional call of a bird. Minutes ticked by. Maybe he wasn't out there after all. Maybe he had left me tied up here and had gone…to do what? To get supplies? I tried not to think what kind of supplies a man like that would want or need. Or maybe he had left because he had to cover his tracks. Maybe there were people who would notice if he disappeared all of a sudden. Maybe he was making preparations to get away from whatever his regular life was and to come back here, probably at nighttime. Bad things always happened at night, when it was dark.

I suddenly realized that I had no idea what time it was. Allison and I had gotten off the bus just after dark on Saturday, and I had been grabbed right after that. Sunlight filtered faintly through one of the shack's filthy windows. It was daytime, which meant that it had to be at least Sunday. But when on Sunday? Please let it be morning. Please.

Bit by bit it got dimmer inside the shack. It got colder too, and I started to shiver. It wasn't morning after all. It must be Sunday afternoon—probably late Sunday afternoon. Oh my god. If he was waiting until nightfall to return, he would be here soon.

Don't panic. Think. Panicking gets you nowhere. If you think, you have a chance.

If it was Sunday night, my mom had definitely missed me. She definitely knew that something was wrong. And she had definitely called the police. That was all good. But then what? Had the police recruited volunteers to look for me? If they had, where were they looking? Where was I?

Minutes crept by, and still the man didn't return. It got gloomier inside the shack. I had to do something before it was too late.

I struggled with the ropes around my wrists and ankles, but they were too tight. My mouth was dry.

My stomach rumbled. My head still felt like it was stuffed with cotton. But I couldn't let any of that distract me. I had to focus on one thing and one thing only—escape.

I looked around the shack. Judging from the layer of dust on the small cast-iron stove that stood against one wall, no one had been here recently. Cobwebs filled the corners below the ceiling and hung like lace from the two rickety shelves on the wall. Mouse droppings speckled the torn, stained mattress that lay crooked on top of a wooden sleeping platform behind me. There were more mouse droppings on the floor below.

My eyes went back to the shelves. One held a metal bowl, a cracked and grimy glass, and a couple of plates. I wondered if there was some cutlery some-where. I wondered if there was a knife.

I didn't see one.

I studied every inch of the inside of the shack. It had been roughly built out of six-inch planks nailed to two-by-four uprights. It didn't appear to be insulated, which told me that whoever it belonged to used it primarily in the summer, although the stove might keep it warm enough in the spring and fall. Maybe it was a hunting cabin. I shuddered at the thought. Hunters have guns. Hunters like to kill.

Don't think about that, I told myself sternly. *Think about how to get out of here. Stay calm. Concentrate.*

I ran my tongue over the rough interior of my mouth. What I wouldn't do for a sip of water. I imagined myself cupping my hands and raising icy stream or lake water to my lips. I imagined it tasting like liquid honey.

Steph, focus! You want water? First find a way out of here—and fast.

I scanned the interior of the shack again. This time, instead of just looking, I focused on seeing. There's a big difference. You can look without really seeing. That's what my grandpa told me the first time he took me on a hike in the woods and I complained about how boring it was, nothing but stupid old trees everywhere. He showed me how to see that all those trees were like the beams of a gigantic building and that there was a whole extended family of creatures—animals, plants, insects, reptiles—making a life in that building. He showed me a lot of other things too. My heart slowed a little. I was able to breathe again. Thinking about Grandpa always made me feel better. I made myself see the shack the way Grandpa would see a meadow or a streambed.

I started at one corner and surveyed the place systematically with my eyes. I was three-quarters of the way around and losing hope when I spotted them: the pointed ends of three—no, four—rusty nails protruding from a couple of two-by-four uprights to which were nailed some newer-looking planks. It looked like someone had repaired a hole or some damaged wood but had done a sloppy job. And that was good for me. If I could position myself in front of one of the rusty nails, maybe I could work the rope against the pointed end until it broke. Maybe.

It took a few agonizing minutes to half drag and half push myself to the closest nail. My legs and hands were numb. I hoped it was because of the cold and not because the ropes were so tight that they were cutting off my circulation. It took several more precious minutes to position myself so that I could start digging the end of the nail into the rope that bound my hands and ankles together. It was a lot harder than I had expected. I kept losing the end of the nail, and because I couldn't see behind me, I couldn't always tell if the nail was hitting the rope at the right place. The whole time I was working on that, I worried that whoever had taken me would walk through the door.

My arms started to ache from being forced into an unnatural position. What if this didn't work? What if I couldn't free myself?

I worked more frantically—and let out a yowl. Something sharp bit into my wrist. The nail. I felt something warm and wet. Maybe it was sweat. But what if it was blood? What if the rusty nail had punctured my skin? You could get tetanus from rusty nails. You could die.

All the more reason to get out of here, I told myself. It was slowly getting dark inside the cabin. The sun would be down soon. I fought back panic as I worked the nail methodically against the rope, but I couldn't make my brain be quiet. What if I couldn't untie myself? What if I died on the floor of this old shack?

Then a miracle happened. The rope that tied my wrists to my ankles gave way.

My wrists were still tied together. So were my ankles. But for the first time I felt hopeful. I had made it this far. I could make it even farther.

I wrestled myself into a sitting position and stretched my stiff legs out in front of me. I wiggled my toes. It felt good. I took a deep breath. Then slowly, painfully, I worked my tied wrists down my back until I could sit on them. *If I could just lift my butt...There!*

I wriggled my wrists under my butt and then wrestled them down further. I bent my knees and pulled them close to me as I worked the rope under my legs, then my feet, then, finally, brought my wrists up in front of me. It was progress.

I turned around and used the nail like a hard, straight finger to loosen the knots in the rope. Now that I could see what I was doing, it went much faster. A few minutes later, victory! My wrists were free. I wriggled my fingers until the circulation returned. Then I untied my ankles.

I struggled to my feet and staggered to the door of the shack. It wasn't locked. It opened, and I peeked outside. My spirits crashed. There was nothing out there but shadowy trees for as far as I could see.

I had no idea where I was.

FOUR

If I had found myself in the same situation in the middle of nowhere a couple of years ago, I would have simply opened that door and run. I wouldn't have cared which direction I went in. All I would have cared about was getting as far away from that shack as fast as possible.

But this wasn't a couple of years ago. This was now, and I knew better. I knew I had to keep my wits about me. I didn't just want to get away; I wanted to get home. For that, I needed a plan.

The first thing I had to do was orient myself.

I walked into the woods as far as I could while still keeping the shack in sight as a point of reference. I figured that whoever had brought me here must have come by car or truck, so I made a wide loop around the shack, looking for signs of a road, a path, even tire tracks. I didn't find anything.

I looked for a lake or a stream, something that I could follow that might take me somewhere.

But all I found were more trees.

I noticed that the land rose to a hill in the distance, but like the terrain around it, the hill was densely wooded.

The sun sank below the tips of the tallest trees. It wouldn't be long before it was completely dark.

I made my way back to the shack and searched it again, using my hands as well as my eyes this time. Besides the dishes I had seen, I found a battered utensil set: a knife, fork and spoon that snapped together. I set them aside. I found half a ball of string, two safety pins and an old metal canteen that looked as if it had survived one of the world wars, probably the first one. I set those aside too. I looked for food, but there was none. I hesitated when I came across a ratty moth-eaten blanket. I was still wearing what I had worn to the city: jeans, sneakers, a long-sleeved T-shirt and a light jacket. It wasn't nearly enough to keep me warm, especially at night. I shook out the blanket and rolled it up. The only other things

I found that could potentially be useful were a length of rope and a thick sheet of filmy plastic. I hunted for matches, a flashlight, a lighter—anything that would let me start a fire or see in the dark—but had no luck.

I put the utensil set, the safety pins and the string in my pocket and wrapped the canteen and the blanket in the plastic. At the last minute, I added a metal bowl. I tied the bundle with the rope, leaving a loop that was long enough to serve as a shoulder strap.

The sun had dropped even lower by the time I had finished, but I didn't let that stop me. I opened the shack's solid door and stepped outside.

They say that when you're lost in the woods and don't know where you are, the smartest thing you can do is to stay put. They say it improves your chances of being found. But staying put wouldn't help me. I wasn't lost because I had taken a wrong turn or stumbled off a trail. I was lost because someone had taken me and tied me up out here—someone who probably intended to kill me. Staying put was the worst thing I could have done.

A three-quarters-full moon peeked out from a cloud-scattered night sky. In its silvery light, I could make out where the rise in the land was. I walked toward it and climbed steadily uphill.

I kept my eyes on the ground and moved as fast as I could. Even though I was doing my best to watch where I was going, I tripped dozens of times on tree roots and rocks that lay hidden by the darkness blanketing the forest floor.

I heard rustling somewhere off to my left. My heart slammed to a stop. It was early spring. Bears had come out of hibernation. I knew there were bears in the area near where I lived—they hung around the edges of the dump outside of town. What if there were bears out here too? Bears that were ravenous after a winter-long sleep? I peered into the blackness around me but saw nothing. Something skittered in the darkness to my left. I stifled a scream and waited, paralyzed. Whatever it was, it fell silent. I told myself it was a chipmunk or a squirrel and that it had disappeared into the woods somewhere. Even so, I couldn't make my legs move. When I finally got going again, I walked more slowly, staring out at the darkness around me, looking for signs of danger.

I was hungrier and thirstier than I had ever been, and my head still felt fuzzy, but I forced myself to keep going. I was panting by the time I allowed myself to sink down onto the trunk of a fallen tree to catch my breath. I gave myself only a few minutes to rest. I had to get to the top of the hill while it was still dark. I might be able to see something up there. And I might be able to find a place to hide.

My mouth was so dry that it hurt to swallow, but I finally made it to the top. It felt good to be away from that shack. I made my way across the crest of the hill to where the land started to fall again and looked out over the shadowy landscape below. I'd been hoping to see lights twinkling in the distance—streetlights marking a major road or highway, lights in buildings in a nearby town, even lights from a lone house. But I saw nothing except the moon-kissed tops of trees, trees and more trees. I was so disappointed that I wanted to cry. Instead I forced myself to circle the crest of the hill, taking care to watch my footing.

I was halfway around when I stopped and blinked. My heart raced with excitement. There was a glow in the distance, like a film of golden light shimmering on the horizon. I couldn't even guess how far away it was—for sure it was far enough that I couldn't reach it in a single night—but there was no doubt in my mind about the source of the glow. It was the light from a distant town or a city. All I had to do was walk toward it.

I wanted to set out right away, but I made myself stop and think first. If I walked down the hill and into the woods again, I would lose sight of the glow. Without a marker to guide me, I would almost certainly drift off course and end up walking in a completely different direction. I looked up at the sky. A few stars were visible among the clouds, but I didn't recognize any of them. Besides, in ten minutes or half an hour or an hour, they would probably be covered by cloud. I hated to admit it— I resisted admitting it—but I had gone as far as I could that night.

I knelt down. My hands trembled as I untied the small bundle I had packed at the shack. I tried not to think that whoever had taken me might have already discovered I was gone. I tried not to think of him as a superhuman tracker who might be climbing up the hill at that very moment to find me and drag me back down to his lair. I fought the urge to run.

I took the ball of string out of my small bundle. I gazed out at the glow—the promise of safety—and tied the string around the trunk of a young tree that stood directly between it and me. Then I made my way carefully down the side of the hill farthest from the shack, hunting in the gloom for a hiding place as I went. Finally, I spotted an outcropping of rock jutting away from the side of the slope like a shelf. I crept under it, spread out my piece of plastic and curled up. I pulled the ratty old blanket over me for warmth and concealment and lay there staring out into the darkness and listening for sounds of danger amidst the whisper of the woods. I was too keyed up to sleep. What if a bear found me? Or a wolf?

Or whoever had taken me?

I kept scanning the terrain around me, even though I couldn't make out anything except vague shapes and shadows. If only I had let Allison's brother drive me home, I would have been safe in my bed. But I had turned down Allison's offer. I had shrugged off her concern. I had walked home alone, in the dark, even though the police had been warning girls for weeks not to do that. I had stood and looked at the field. It had even occurred to me to go the long way around. But I hadn't done that either. I wished I had. Then I never would have run into whoever had grabbed me. Maybe—I'm ashamed to admit I thought this—maybe he would have grabbed someone else instead. Then things would be different.

Or maybe—I shuddered as it occurred to me—they wouldn't have.

Maybe he hadn't been hiding in that field waiting for the next girl careless enough to take a shortcut through it. Maybe he'd planned it all ahead of time. Maybe he'd been watching me for days. Maybe he'd studied my habits and knew the route I usually took to and from school and town. I thought hard. After I left Elgin Street, I hadn't seen another soul. I hadn't heard anything either. Maybe he'd been standing across the street from Ralph's. Maybe he'd seen me get off the bus. Maybe he'd got into his car or truck and had driven on ahead to the field, confident that I'd be along soon. Maybe he'd waited until I was in the field where no one would see me because of the trees and the bushes.

When he'd grabbed me, I'd thought I was going to die. I'd put up a fight—the fight of my life. I'd kicked.

I'd tried to pry him off me. I'd scratched him—at least, I thought I had. Then something had jabbed me in the arm, and here I was.

I shivered under my blanket. I couldn't let him catch me again. I couldn't let him do to me what he had done to those other two girls.

FIVE

I woke up when the sun burst under the ledge that was sheltering me. I was stiff and cold, hungry and thirsty, but I didn't move. Not at first anyway. Instead I lay still and listened to the world beyond. Listened for him. But the only sound I heard was birds twittering and calling from treetops.

I poked my head out and peered around. The woods looked less forbidding in the morning light. Most of the trees closest to me were pine, their straight trunks rising high above the forest floor before their evergreen branches shot out, fighting among themselves for the sun's rays. The forest floor was carpeted with a thick layer of dried brown pine needles through which poked the green spring noses and gangly limbs of dozens of different types of plants. Fallen trees and outcroppings of rock studded the landscape.

I didn't see a soul.

I climbed out from under the rock ledge, my eyes searching the horizon.

Nothing.

My heart hammered in my chest. I reached for the blanket, pulled it out and folded it into the plastic. I started to tie up my small bundle, but there was something I needed to know first. I pulled off my jacket.

Something fell to the ground and sparkled in the morning sun.

I bent down. It was a length of gold chain. Where had that come from?

Then I remembered. When I'd been grabbed from behind, I had kicked and struggled. When I couldn't pry my attacker's arm off my neck, I had reached behind me to try to claw at him, anything to make him let me go. My fingers had closed around something—the chain—and I'd pulled hard. The two end links of the piece of chain on the ground were broken. I must have snapped the chain when I pulled on it. But how had it gotten into my jacket?

I checked inside. There was a small snag in the jacket lining. The chain must have fallen down inside the back of my jacket and got caught there somehow. I picked it up and tucked it into my jeans pocket. Maybe it would help the police find my kidnapper— assuming I ever made it out of these woods.

I peeled off my T-shirt and did what I'd set out to do: I took a good look at my arm. It wasn't easy to spot, but finally I found it—a tiny puncture mark. I was right. I had been jabbed in the arm with a needle. I was already shivering in the crisp morning air, but the thought that someone had drugged me sent a chill deep into my bones. I put my clothes back on, tied up my bundle and looped the rope over my shoulder. I stared back up the hill, looking for any sign of danger. When I had convinced myself that there was no one up there, I crept back up on my hands and knees, staying as low to the ground as I could.

I took another cautious look around before I stood up and began to hunt for the sapling with the piece of string tied around its trunk. I found it easily and positioned myself so that it was between me and the horizon, just as I had done the night before. It was my marker, my only hope. Now all I had to do was remember what Grandpa had taught me.

Up until two years ago, I had barely known my grandfather, partly because he lived far away, but mostly because my mom didn't approve of him. Grandpa lived in the bush outside a small town way up north. He had retired there after a lifetime working for a mining company. My mom always referred to him as the Hermit. Because of that, I'd imagined him as a crazy, long-bearded old man who lived alone and never saw or spoke to another human being. It turned out he did live alone. But he went into town regularly, and everyone there seemed to know him. He couldn't walk more than a few steps without someone calling out hello and wanting to know how he'd been since his last trip in for supplies. He worked sporadically, guiding tourists who wanted a wilderness experience or, one time, a film production company that was shooting some scenes for an action-adventure movie. Most of the time, though, he just enjoyed the peace and quiet.

Despite my mother's disapproval of him, two years ago, she announced that she wanted me to go and stay with him for the summer. I fought with her when she told me her plans. I said I didn't want to spend one day, let alone a whole summer, with a crazy old hermit I barely knew in the middle of the dirty old woods, which I hated even though I had never spent any time in them. Needless to say, I lost the fight. As soon as school was over, I was loaded onto a bus that I'm positive had been a school bus in a previous incarnation and was shipped north to a town I couldn't have located on a map if my life had depended on it. My stomach churned the whole way. I knew my grandfather liked being alone. I knew he preferred silence. My dad told me that his father never could abide mindless chatter. Was he going to expect me to keep my mouth shut all summer? Thinking about that made me mad. I hadn't asked to waste my whole summer with him, so who did he think he was, demanding complete and utter silence, like I was a cloistered nun? What if he didn't even want me there? What if he'd been coerced into taking me because, after all, I was his granddaughter?

He turned out to be as quiet as my dad had said he was. He didn't have a TV or a computer, although he did have a radio that he could use to reach the fire tower and the closest police detachment, just in case. When he wasn't working or hiking, he read.

Boy, did he read. All of his trips into town included either a trip to the library or a visit to the post office to pick up packages of books he had ordered by mail. He encouraged me to read too, and I did. What choice did I have? It was either that or sit around and stare at trees all day. He taught me how to cook and bake outdoors. He took me on canoe trips. And we went hiking. Sometimes we'd be gone for days with only a backpack and sleeping bag each, and a small tarp that Grandpa would pitch over us to keep us dry. It turned out to be the best summer of my life.

Before I left, I made plans to go back the next summer. But by late that winter, Grandpa was gone. He had a heart attack. I guess it had come on fast because he didn't radio anyone. We found out after someone in town remarked to someone else that he hadn't seen Grandpa in a while. When it turned out that no one had, a constable was dispatched to his cabin by snowmobile. By the time he got there, Grandpa had been dead for weeks. "That's what comes of being a hermit," my mom said when they told her what had happened. I cried for days. He had taught me so much…

Like how to use the sun as a compass.

I gathered some twigs and used three of them to make an arrow pointing directly at the sapling with the string tied around it and at the horizon beyond. Then I found a small clearing on the ground that was bathed in sunlight, and I planted the longest, straightest stick in the ground in the middle of it. When the sun caught the stick, it cast a shadow. I slipped off my watch and set it on the ground so that the hour hand pointed toward and along the shadow cast by the stick. Then I pictured an imaginary line running across the watch halfway between the hour hand and twelve o'clock. That's your north-south line, Grandpa had told me. South is between the hour hand and twelve o'clock. North is the opposite direction. Once I had found north and south, I also knew where east and west were.

I looked at the arrow I had made pointing toward the glow I had seen the night before. According to my compass, it was due west from the sapling. All I had to do was walk west in a straight line and I would eventually reach those lights. I had no idea how far I would have to walk or how long it would take. I hoped I would have the chance to find out. But first I had two more pressing problems to deal with. One, I had to get moving and stay moving before my kidnapper came looking for me. Two, I had to find water. A person could go a long time without food but not without water. And as near as I could figure, it had been more than thirty-six hours since I had had anything to drink. My mouth was dry. My tongue felt heavy and swollen. All I could think of was water.

I looked up at the sky. It was clear blue. The clouds that had covered the stars only hours ago had vanished. There seemed to be no chance that it was going to rain anytime soon, and I sure wasn't going to find any water up here.

I circled the crest of the hill again, careful to keep my only landmark—the sapling with the twine wrapped around it—in sight. I peered down and through the trees until my eyes hurt, but I didn't see a stream, a lake or even a puddle.

I made my way back to the sapling, peered due west into the forest and picked out two distinctive trees. One was a pine tree with a dead branch jutting out from one side. The other, farther along but in the same line as the pine, was a birch that had been split almost in half, probably by lightning. If I kept my eyes on both trees and walked directly toward them, I would be going in the right direction. I removed the string from the trunk of the sapling and threw the sticks I had gathered into the scrub. I set off down the hill.

As I walked, my eyes skipped from the two trees, scanning for any sign of water—a small natural spring, a creek, anything that I hadn't been able to see from up above. Every time I passed an outcropping of rocks, I checked for indentations. Rain water could pool in those indentations, Grandpa had told me. If the indentations were deep enough and it had rained hard enough, it might take a long time for the water to evaporate.

I walked and walked, daydreaming about water the way I used to daydream about ice-cream sundaes on hot summer days when I was a little kid. I passed small rocks, large rocks, massive rocks. Nothing. I scanned the forest floor for any sign of moisture that might indicate a spring. I walked until my idea of paradise was an image of myself bent over a sink, my mouth under a running faucet as water—icy cold water—streamed down my throat. What I wouldn't give…And I kept checking my tree markers to make sure that I wasn't veering off course. Every few minutes I stopped and held my breath and listened for even the smallest of sounds that might signal that someone was following me. Each time I started to breathe again, a tremor ran through me. Just because I didn't hear anything didn't mean someone wasn't out there tracking me.

The ground under my feet sloped downward. Halfway down the slope, a massive outcropping, probably deposited by a retreating glacier millions of years ago, loomed up from the forest floor. As I trudged toward it, I saw something shimmering. I hardly dared to hope. If you don't hope, you won't be disappointed, right? What I was seeing was probably the sun reflecting off some mineral embedded in the rock. Or maybe—it wouldn't surprise me—it was a mirage, like in a movie when some poor guy is dying of thirst out in the desert and suddenly he sees a huge pool of cool, clear, deliciously wet water with people frolicking in it, as if they were in a five-star resort. The guy runs to the side of the pool and starts scooping the water into his mouth with both hands. Then the mirage vanishes and you see that he's eating sand instead of drinking water.

The closer I got, the bigger the rock outcropping looked, until, by the time I got there, I saw that it was twice as tall as me. If I wanted to find out what was glistening in the sun, I would have to clamber up the side to take a look, and what was the point? I was already exhausted. Besides, it was probably nothing.

On the other hand, it might be something. It might be water.

I found a foothold in the rock face and started to pull myself up, my feet searching for footholds in the rock face. When I finally hoisted myself to the top, my heart skipped a beat. There was a bowl-like indentation in the middle of the highest rock. Cradled in the indentation was a puddle of water.

I hauled myself up onto that rock and knelt beside the puddle.

I had no idea how long it had been there or what might have fallen into it or leeched into it from the rock. Grandpa always said that you should assume water was unsafe to drink unless you knew for certain that it wasn't. He said that before you drink unsafe water, you have to purify it by either boiling it or adding water purification tablets to it. I couldn't do either. I had nothing to start a fire with and no purification tablets. I stared down at the shallow layer of water. If I drank it and it wasn't safe, I could get sick. I could even die. On the other hand, if I didn't drink something soon, I could also die.

I decided to take my chances.

I bent down until my lips touched the surface of the water and drank greedily. It wasn't long before I had drunk the puddle dry. I stayed where I was for a few moments, waiting to see if I was going to start writhing in pain. But I felt okay.

I lowered myself off the rock and checked my landmarks again. They were harder to make out now, and I knew that the farther down the slope I walked, the more difficult it would be to keep them in sight. I needed new markers. I searched for two more distinctive trees along the same westerly line and settled on a massive cedar with a patch of brown near the top and two birches, the second leaning on the first. As I trudged toward them, I searched for more water.

My stomach growled. I hadn't eaten in nearly two whole days. Whenever I had gone hiking or camping with Grandpa, we had taken food with us. Sometimes we picked berries and ate them, but this was only April. It was too early for berries. Sometimes Grandpa caught fish or trapped small animals and cooked them. But how could I catch a fish when there was no stream or lake around? How could I trap an animal without a trap or anything to make one from?

I was hungry, but I also knew that people could live for a surprisingly long time without food. Still, while I walked, I imagined all the things I would eat when I finally got home: pepperoni pizza with extra cheese, my mom's chicken-and-rice casserole, a frosty vanilla milkshake, warm fresh bread from Alice's bakery on Dundas Street. My mouth watered.

SIX

I picked out landmark after landmark and plodded on. My legs ached. My head ached. What I really wanted to do was curl up under a tree and go to sleep. But if I didn't keep moving, I would never reach my destination. Worse, whoever had taken me might find me and drag me back to that shack. I forced myself to go on. I walked until the sun began to dip in the sky. By the time I finally stumbled into a meadow, my legs as heavy as lead, I was lightheaded from lack of food and water, and the sky had changed from the blue of daytime to the yellow and orange of dusk. Once the sun was down, I wouldn't be able to orient myself properly. I would have to stay put for the night.

Now that I had to stop, I didn't want to. What if the man who had drugged me and brought me to that shack was a hunter? What if he knew how to track animals? If you can track animals, you can track people, right? What if he knew these woods like that back of his hand? What if he could track me even in the dark? What if he crept up on me while I was sleeping? What if…?

Stop it, Steph. Stop it right now.

When you get lost in the woods, Grandpa had told me, your number one enemy is panic. Panic makes you think of all the things that *could* happen. A grizzly could attack you. You could starve to death. You could freeze to death. You could die of thirst. You could stay lost forever. You could die out there. Thoughts like that are what cause people to panic, and when people panic, they do things they shouldn't. They keep moving when they should stop. They walk in the dark instead of waiting for the light and the sun. They reason that if they keep walking, even if they can't see where they're going, they'll get *somewhere*. But what they usually end up doing is walking in circles or stepping into a hole and breaking an ankle or tripping over a rock or a tree trunk and breaking something else. They forget every piece of good sense they ever had—assuming they had any to begin with. Grandpa said he was dismayed by most people's lack of knowledge of the outdoors. They would never get behind the wheel of a car without learning the rules of the road, he said. But they strolled out into the woods without knowing the first thing about orienting themselves or about what to touch and what to avoid. He made sure I knew those things. He also taught me what steps to take to fight off panic.

First: *Stay positive by taking stock of whatever progress you've made.* On the plus side, I had escaped from the shack. I had found a distant source of help in the distance. I had walked all day toward it. I had found some water—not a lot, but some. I was still alive, unlike the first girl who had been taken. All of that was good. On the minus side, I was hungrier than ever and needed more water. And I was scared. But at least I had accomplished something.

Second: *Confirm your whereabouts as best you can.* Okay, so I had no idea where I was. But I knew where I needed to go, and the sun was still high enough to help me see how I was doing. I hunted around until I found another stick, and I planted it in the ground. I pulled out my watch, checked my direction again, and discovered that I had managed to stay on a more or less westerly course. This was also good. It was very good. I fashioned another arrow out of twigs and pointed it toward my destination so I would know which direction to walk come morning.

Third: *Observe your surroundings to see if you can find anything that can help you.* I looked around. The meadow I was in formed a large circle carved out of the forest. Maybe it was a natural meadow. Or maybe it was a man-made clearing. Maybe it had been a homestead at one time. Grandpa had told me that he had stumbled on lots of places over the years where people had tried to make a go of it. Some had tried to farm. Others had prospected or hunted and trapped. But eventually, because the land was too hard or the settler became ill or died, the land was abandoned. One thing was sure though, he'd said. If someone *had* settled an area at one time or another, that meant there was a water source nearby.

I paced the meadow methodically, looking for any evidence that a cabin or house had once stood in it.

I found nothing.

Nothing but wild grasses and weeds.

I glanced back over my shoulder. The stick I had planted in the ground to check my direction was taller than the grass around it. Reassured that I would be able to find it again, I set off beyond the edges of the clearing to scout for a water source.

I went as far as I dared in each direction. Still nothing. Either I had stumbled on a natural meadow or someone had found a way to live out here without water. Or they had dug a well, which lay hidden somewhere among the trees and grasses.

I headed back to the meadow. By now the sun had dipped below the treetops, and the meadow was filled with shadows. My legs ached even more, my feet were sorer than ever and I felt sick and weak from hunger. I had to make camp for the night. But should I sleep in the open meadow, or would I be safer sheltered in the woods? I settled on a compromise. I spread my sheet of plastic on the ground under a tree near the edge of the clearing, curled up on it and pulled the moth-eaten blanket over me. I lay there, every nerve ending alive to the possibility of danger, and wondered about whoever had taken me.

Where had he gone after leaving me in that shack? What exactly had he been planning to do to me? What had he done to those other girls? Had he returned to the shack yet? Had he found me missing? If so, what was he doing about it? Had he shrugged off my escape? It was possible. After all, I hadn't seen his face. I had no idea who he was. Maybe he was confident that even if I managed to make it to safety, I posed no threat. Maybe he was on the move at this very minute, looking for another town where another fourteen-year-old girl was on her way home alone. Or maybe he knew something about these woods that I didn't. Maybe he knew that I didn't have a chance of making it out.

Or—the thought made my empty stomach churn—what if he had taken me to that shack and had backed off to wait for me to escape? What if that was his thing—what if he was a psycho who liked to hunt people? I knew that the first girl who had vanished had been found in the woods some-where, but I didn't know which woods. I also didn't know what condition she'd been in. Had she been trying to escape like me? Had she been hungry and thirsty and scared? Had he been tracking her, maybe getting close enough to watch her and see the fear and panic in her eyes? Had he finally closed in on her and...?

What if he was watching me now? What if he was waiting for me to fall asleep?

All my senses were on full alert. My ears strained for any sound. My eyes searched the trees, the rocks, the bushes. I sniffed the air and wished I had the scenting abilities of a dog or a bear. I struggled to stay awake. A loud snap somewhere in the woods behind me propelled me bolt upright, my heart pounding. In the moments that followed, it felt as if everything had vanished except me and whatever, or whoever, had made that noise.

I told myself it was nothing, maybe just a dead branch falling to the forest floor. Or maybe an animal.

Maybe a large animal. Maybe a bear. Or a wolf. Were there wolves in these woods? I started to shake all over. Wolves traveled in packs. They could be ferocious.

Somehow during the night—I have no idea how—I fell asleep.

The sun woke me, and instinctively my whole body tensed. I listened for a moment, but all I heard was the chirping of birds overhead and all around. I opened my eyes. If there was anyone out there, I didn't see him. I stretched my aching body and peered out into the meadow. If things had been different, if I had been there with my grandpa instead of all alone, I might have thought I was in some kind of Eden. The long grass in the meadow sparkled with what looked like tiny diamonds. It was the sun hitting and reflecting off the dew that had appeared while I slept.

Dew.

I sat up and stared at the droplets that studded each stalk of grass.

Dew...

Water.

I jumped up, ran to the edge of the meadow and flung myself down onto my hands and knees to lick the grass. The moisture was cool and sweet on my parched tongue. I licked some more. As I crawled through the grass, I noticed that my movements were making most of the moisture fall to the ground. I knew, thanks to Grandpa, that it wouldn't be long before the heat from the sun evaporated all those precious droplets. What could I do? Was there some way I could collect the dew? I sat back on my knees to think. That's when I noticed that the wrists of my jacket and the thighs of my jeans were soaking wet.

That gave me an idea.

I ripped off my jacket and pulled off my T-shirt. Then I put my jacket back on and stared at the shirt. I hated to sacrifice it, but if I was going to do this, I would have to be quick, and I couldn't think of a faster way. I bit into the hem until I made a small tear. Then I grasped the shirt with both hands and ripped it in half. I tied a T-shirt half around each ankle, stood up and waded through the damp grass. It wasn't long before both halves of the T-shirt were soaked through.

I walked back to where I had left my few supplies, untied the T-shirt halves and wrung them out into the metal bowl I had packed. Then I carefully poured the water from the bowl into the metal canteen. I screwed on the top and waded into the meadow again. Back and forth I went, soaking up the dew, wringing it out into the bowl and pouring the water into the canteen until—a miracle—I heard a satisfying sloshing sound when I shook it. I kept going until I had harvested every bit of dew I could find. Finally I sank down to my knees, raised the bowl to my lips and drank every drop that wouldn't fit into the canteen. It was delicious.

I felt a little better. I had satisfied my thirst and still had water to carry with me. I retied my bundle, checked my direction, located two new landmarks and set off toward the west again. At least I wouldn't die of thirst—not today anyway.

SEVEN

My stomach rumbled and grumbled and groaned. As I stumbled through the woods, I thought about food—roast turkey and gravy, chicken and dumplings, Grandpa's fresh-caught fish pan-fried over an open fire, the biscuits he made some mornings that we ate hot with butter and Grandpa's homemade jam. What I wouldn't give for just one mouthful of biscuit and jam.

Or at least something to chew on.

The pine forest slowly gave way to a variety of trees. There were more birches and, every now and then, a patch of cedar. I gazed thoughtfully at the birches and remembered Grandpa asking me, "Did you know, Stephanie, that spaghetti grows on trees?"

Right. Like I was going to believe that.

"No, it doesn't, Grandpa, Spaghetti is made from wheat, and wheat grows in fields, not on trees."

"I'm not talking about spaghetti and meatballs. I'm talking about wilderness spaghetti."

"Wilderness spaghetti?" Uh-oh. Here we go again, I thought. Grandpa's conversation was full of wilderness this and wilderness that. "You're telling me that wilderness spaghetti grows on trees?"

"Yup."

He sounded serious. I pictured a tree that looked something like a maple tree, but with big strings of spaghetti hanging from it, like the leaves and branches of a weeping willow made out of pasta. I described it to Grandpa. He laughed.

"You find wilderness spaghetti on the inside of the tree, Stephanie, not the outside."

It turned out that the wilderness spaghetti that Grandpa was talking about was the inner bark of a birch tree.

"You can eat it," he said. "When you cut it into strips and add it to soup or stew, you can't tell that it's not real spaghetti. If you have to, you can eat it raw."

"Yuck!" I said.

But that was then. Now I stared at every birch I passed and wondered if Grandpa had been telling the truth or pulling my leg. Finally I stopped. I ran my hand over the papery outer bark of a young birch. It was true that Grandpa liked silence. But when he talked, he told old-fashioned jokes and funny stories about people he had known—mostly people he had guided through the bush. All of those stories, funny as they were, had a lesson to them, and usually the lesson was about being careful, being prepared and staying calm—in other words, about surviving. Grandpa never joked about surviving.

I dug the metal utensil set out of my pocket and unsnapped the knife. It wasn't very sharp, but by pressing hard—so hard that the end of the knife handle dug deep into the palm of my hand—I managed to make two longish parallel cuts in the bark. Then I made two shorter cuts joining the two longer cuts and peeled back the outer bark. I worked the knife deeper into the tree and peeled off a piece of the pale inner bark. I held it to my nose and sniffed. It smelled like tree. I bit off a tiny piece. It was like biting into soft, thin leather. I chewed carefully. It tasted faintly sweet, but chewing it was like chewing the sole of a ballet slipper.

It took forever before it was soft enough to swallow. I ate another, slightly larger, piece. My stomach continued to grumble and growl, but I made myself wait to see if I was going to throw up or get stomach cramps or double up in agony.

Nothing bad happened.

I made more cuts in the birch tree and peeled off more bark, which I jammed into my mouth. I worked for what seemed like a long time, digging, cutting, peeling and chewing the whole time, until the grumbling in my belly stopped and I had extra pieces of bark in my pocket to eat later.

I set off into the morning.

A few hours later, when I came to another small clearing, I stopped and quickly checked my direction again. Then I walked. I walked all day. I walked until the sun began to set directly ahead of me, confirmation that I was headed in the right direction. Then I looked around for a place to sleep for the night.

This time I found no meadow, no clearing, no chance of collecting more dew. I looked for the biggest tree with the smoothest ground beneath it. After I made an arrow out of twigs and pointed it westward so that I would be able to orient myself in the morning, I gathered up armfuls of pine needles for a mattress. I spread my sheet of plastic over top of them and lay down. It wasn't even close to my comfy bed back home, but at least it was better than the hard ground. I wrapped myself in the blanket, drank the last of the water from the canteen and curled into a ball to make myself as small and unnoticeable as possible.

The minute my body stopped working, my brain kicked in. Would tonight be the night that a pack of wolves would find me? Would a bear catch my scent and come to investigate? Was *he* out there looking for me?

Who was he anyway?

What did he look like? What did he do for a living? Did people who knew him have even the slightest suspicion about his secret life? What made him do what he did?

What exactly had he done to those other girls?

If only I had listened to my mom.

If only I had done what she'd told me.

If only I hadn't been so mad at her.

If only my last words to her hadn't been angry ones.

When I'd left the house on Saturday morning and she had told me to be careful, I'd yelled back at her.

"I hope he catches me," I'd said. "I hope he catches me and kills me. I'd rather be dead than have to listen to you and Gregg every night."

My mom's face had turned crimson, and I'd felt a rush of victory. I'd been trying to hurt her, and I had succeeded. It hadn't occurred to me until now how she must have felt when I'd said that to her—and how she might feel now. Did she feel responsible for what had happened to me? Was she blaming herself?

Or—there it was again, the chill of panic radiating out from my spine and down my arms and legs to my fingers and toes—did she think I'd run away again? Did she think I was trying to get back at her? Was she sitting at home right now, waiting for me to finally break down and call her or maybe, as I'd done before, walk through the door, still filled with anger and resentment?

Was she glad I was gone, at least for a while? I'd been such a pain lately. Maybe she didn't miss me at all. Maybe she was relieved that she didn't have to listen to my rants about Gregg. Maybe she was as angry with me as I was with her.

※

I had been angry with my mom for a long time.

It started one day when my father was driving home from the city. He traveled back and forth a couple of times a month for meetings. Before each trip, he always went to the library and checked out a couple of books on tape. "If I'm going to be trapped in my car for a few hours each way, I might as well put my time to good use," he said. He never listened to fiction books. He always chose something more serious—history or politics.

I'd pictured it a hundred times—my dad tooling along the highway, nodding slightly to the tape like he always did when he was trying to concentrate. He was watching the traffic too and being careful to keep the correct distance between his car and the one ahead of him. My father never tailgated—"If you're too close to the car in front of you, you won't be able to stop safely if anything happens," he always said. My dad was a very careful man.

He checked his rearview mirror regularly too.

If anyone was tailgating him, he always pulled into the right lane to let whoever it was get past him.

Maybe he glanced into the three lanes of traffic going in the other direction on the other side of the median, but probably he didn't. What happened over there didn't matter, not to a careful driver. It was all about what was happening on your side of the median. My dad had no patience for people who slowed down to look at accidents on the other side of the road. He called those people rubberneckers.

If I'm right, if he kept his eyes on the traffic directly in front of him and behind him, then he probably hadn't noticed the massive eighteen-wheel truck that was barreling along in the right lane on the other side of the median. He probably hadn't seen that one of its enormous tires was wobbling crazily. He hadn't seen when that tire finally came loose from the truck. In fact, according to the police traffic experts who had made all kinds of measurements of skid marks and distances, he probably hadn't seen the tire fly away from the truck at 150 kilometers an hour. He hadn't seen it hit the six-inch-high concrete divider that marked the grass-filled median. He hadn't seen it bounce up into the air right after that.

At about the same time that the truck lost its tire, I was walking home from school with Allison, hoping my mom would be out when we got there. We liked to have the place to ourselves so that we could do whatever we wanted without my mom always asking, "What are you two up to?" But my mom wasn't out. She was in the kitchen, getting supper started.

"Hi, girls," she said cheerily as we came through the door.

"Hi, Mrs. Rawls," Allison said. She was always polite.

Not me.

I ignored my mom. I grabbed a bag of chips from the cupboard and a couple of sodas from the fridge, and I dragged Allison upstairs before my mom could trap her in a conversation.

We were in my room until five thirty, when Allison had to go home for supper. While I was seeing her out, a car pulled into our driveway. A police car. My mom must have heard tires crunching on the gravel because she called, "Is that your father?"

"It's the cops," I said. I remember thinking, What are they even doing here? Stupid cops, they must have the wrong address.

My mom came to the door, wiping her hands on her apron. The expression on her face startled me. She looked worried.

It wasn't just any cop who showed up at our door. It was Clark Adderly, the chief of police. He came up the walk and onto the porch.

"Evening, Trish," he said, removing his hat. "Stephanie."

I don't know if it was the sad look in his eyes or whether the worry I'd seen on my mom's face was contagious, but I got a sick feeling in my stomach.

"I'm afraid I have some bad news for you, Trish," he said. "Can I come in?"

From what he said and from what the traffic experts later confirmed, my dad probably hadn't seen that truck tire flying directly at his car until it was too late to do anything about it. It hit my father's windshield head-on and smashed right through the glass. My father's car veered out of control. The car immediately behind him swerved to avoid him. The car in the lane next to him swerved too. Cars behind my dad's car slammed on their brakes. Miraculously, no one was hurt.

No one except my dad.

His car kept moving after the tire crashed through the windshield. It finally ran right off the road and into a ditch. A number of drivers called 9-1-1 on their cell phones. The police and the paramedics arrived. It took them three hours to pry my father out from under the truck tire. But it didn't matter. According to the pathologist, he'd been killed on impact. My careful father was dead, and my whole life changed.

EIGHT

When I was in grade five, Megan Campbell's father died. It wasn't an accident like what happened to my dad. Megan's father had cancer. Megan didn't come to school for a whole week. When she finally showed up again, she kept her head down most of the time and stood by herself in the playground at recess. I didn't know her very well, so I never went over to her and talked to her or anything. After a couple of weeks, one of the girls I hung out with said, "She should just get over it already." Another girl said, "He was going to die anyway." And, after a while, Megan did seem to get over it. At least, that's what it looked like. She started participating in class again and hung around with a couple of other girls at lunch and recess. She seemed normal instead of being poor sad Megan. It never occurred to me what it must have been like at her house after her father died. In fact, I never gave a second thought to her—until my dad died. Then I wondered: Is this what Megan went through? Is this how she felt?

After Clark Adderly left our house that night, I felt like someone had ripped open my heart and stuffed it full of all the things people never want to feel: grief and pain and hurt and sorrow. I thought I would never stop crying. I stayed away from school for two whole weeks. When I went back, I didn't want to talk to anyone—well, except Allison. Cindy Houghton came up to me outside school before the early bell and said she was sorry about my dad. Right there, in front of everyone who was waiting around before they had to go inside, I started to cry. No one came up to me after that. No one said anything at all to me about my dad after that day. I guess they were all afraid I was going to cry. If it hadn't been for Allison, who stuck to me the whole time and who never freaked when I got all weepy, I don't know what I would have done.

It wasn't any better at home. My mom wept—not cried, but *wept*—for days. She wept when Clark Adderly told her the news. She wept all that night. She wept the next morning when two of her closest friends came over to help her with "the arrangements." They had to hold her up at the funeral. Over the next few weeks, she lost a ton of weight. She barely ate and couldn't sleep unless she took a heavy-duty sleeping pill. She was a mess. I thought a lot about Megan Campbell.

I found out later from my grandpa, who had come for the funeral, that my mom hadn't called him about me. Instead he had called her and offered to take me for the summer: "To give you a chance to pull yourself together, Trish." My mom refused at first. She didn't want to send me up there alone, but her friends said they thought it would be a good idea: "Not just for you, Trish, but for Stephanie too. She's hurting too. Maybe getting away for a while will be good for her." So off I went for nearly three months.

When I got home again, my mom had stopped crying. She had met Gregg.

They met at a support group that my mom's friends had dragged her to. Gregg's wife had died the year before, also in an accident. He and my mom spent the summer going to weekly group meetings in the church hall where people talked about their dead loved ones and how lost they felt without them. According to Allison, who overheard it from her mom, who, as a hairdresser, heard all the best gossip in town, it wasn't long before my mom and Gregg started having coffee together after group. Then dinner. Then...well, you get the idea. I couldn't believe it.

At Thanksgiving that year, Gregg sat at my father's place at the dining room table and carved the turkey. Right after that, he started showing up for supper a couple of times a week. And staying the night. He didn't out-and-out move in with us; it was more like he was doing it by stealth. His shaving stuff took over one of the little shelves in the shower. He left a change of clothes at our house, "just in case." Then a couple of changes of clothes. His dirty jeans and T-shirts showed up in the laundry. He started keeping his run book on the little desk in the corner of the kitchen where the phone was, and he would sit there after supper some nights, figuring out how many runs he had made to fill those vending machines and how many miles he had driven so that he could bill his buddy.

Half the time when I answered the phone, it was someone calling for Gregg. It was right about then that my mom and I started fighting. I told her that no one was going to replace my dad, ever. I told her that people were talking about her. I told her that she must not have loved my father if she could start seeing someone else so soon after he died. When I said that, she slapped me. I was so surprised, so hurt and so angry with her that I took off, just like that. I hated her. I didn't want to be around her anymore. I walked out to the highway and stuck out my thumb. I wasn't even sure where I was going— north, I guess, to my grandpa. But anywhere would have been fine, so long as it was away from my mom.

Mr. Whitten, the director of the choir at the church we went to, pulled over and picked me up. He asked me where I was going. I said I had to visit a friend in the next town. He dropped me there, and I stuck out my thumb again. The second car that picked me up was a police car with Clark Adderly at the wheel. It turned out that Mr. Whitten had been worried about me and had called the police. Clark Adderly drove me home. When he told my mom where he had found me, she started to cry.

Didn't I realize how dangerous it was to hitchhike? Didn't I know that I could get killed? I screamed at her that I didn't care.

I ran away a few more times after that. Every time I did, my mom freaked out. Every time I got home again, she cried. But it didn't change anything. She kept seeing Gregg. He spent more and more time at our house. Two days before I was taken, she told me that she and Gregg had started talking about maybe getting married.

"Married?" I couldn't believe it. "It's only been two years since Dad died. How can you think about getting married? I thought you loved Dad."

"I did," my mom said. "I still do."

"No, you don't. You love Gregg."

"That doesn't mean I don't love your father too. I'll always love him." Her eyes got all teary, but she wasn't fooling me. If she had really loved my dad, she wouldn't have started seeing Gregg so soon after he died. She wouldn't be talking about getting married again. "But life goes on, Stephanie."

"Not for Dad, it doesn't."

My mom stiffened.

"I'm thirty-six years old, Stephanie," she said. "You can't expect me to spend the rest of my life alone.

I'll never forget your father. But I can't change the fact that he's gone. And I know he'd want me to be happy. He'd want the same for you."

"I *am* happy. I'm happy with the way things are. But I won't be happy if you try to force a new father on me. He's a mechanic. Dad was an engineer. He was a million times smarter than Gregg."

"Gregg is smart in his own way. He's going to start his own business."

"So he keeps saying." Like *that* was ever going to happen. "It takes money, Mom, not to mention brains, to start a business."

"He has a plan. It looks good."

"But he's broke. You've seen his truck." It was rusted out in a few places, and one of the bumpers had a huge dent in it from when he backed into a utility pole one night after a poker game. "Look at where he lives!" His so-called house was a crummy basement apartment in a six-plex up near the lumberyard. "He can't start a business. He doesn't have any money."

"We're going to be partners," my mom said. She was angry with me now.

I stared at her. She didn't work. She had never worked. She was living off what my father had left her. She'd also received a big settlement from the insurance company—they'd paid double because his death had been accidental—and from a lawsuit she had filed against the trucking company. She had gotten some good advice and had invested it so that it would last. We would be okay. There was even enough set aside to pay for my education. But we still had to be careful. Usually when people were partners in a business, they both put something into it. What was my mom planning to put in?

Suddenly it hit me.

"You're not going to lend Gregg money, are you?" I said. "The money we got from Dad is supposed to look after us. You're not going to throw it away on some business Gregg wants to start, are you?"

She didn't answer, but I knew that was exactly what she was planning to do.

"No way," I said. "No way."

"Stephanie, please. I need you to be okay with this. I need you to say that it's okay with you if Gregg and I get married."

"It's not okay," I said. "And I have rights too. If you try to use that money for Gregg's business, I'll talk to Martin." Martin was a friend of my dad's. He was a lawyer. He had handled my dad's affairs.

"That money is for us, so that we don't have to worry about anything. It isn't for Gregg."

"Stephanie—"

I walked out on her and slammed the door as loudly as I could, but even still, I heard her yell, "You're impossible."

I was impossible? *She* was impossible. I told myself I hated her.

That was then.

Now I would do anything to see her again. Anything. I would even put up with Gregg. He wasn't so bad. He made my mom happy, and I guess that was something. He'd even tried to talk to me one time. He'd sat down on the couch while I was watching TV and he'd said, "I know I could never replace your dad, and I don't want to, Steph. But you and me can be friends, right? I mean, we both care about the same thing. We both care about your mom."

Of course I hadn't even looked at him, much less answered him. But he had tried. He really had. And maybe my mom was right—maybe he was smart in his own way. Just because he wasn't a success now didn't mean he couldn't make a go of it. Maybe he just needed a break. Maybe my mom was that break. She sure seemed to believe in him.

Tears dribbled down my cheeks as I huddled under my ratty old blanket. I wanted to go home. I wanted to *be* home. I would have given anything to have been tucked in my own bed in my own room in my own house. But what if that never happened? What if I never got home? I started to sob.

Pull yourself together, I told myself sternly. *You have to stay positive. You'll never make it if you give up.* I dug into my pocket and pulled out the chain I had found snagged on the inside of my jacket. I was one hundred percent positive that it belonged to the man who had grabbed me. It didn't look like much—there were probably thousands, maybe even millions, of chains just like it. But it might give the police something to go on. It might help them catch the guy. I wiped the tears from my face. *There* was a positive thought to help keep me going: *I* could help the police catch the man who had taken those other two girls. I could help to catch a serial killer. But in order for that to happen, I had to keep going. I had to get back home.

I slipped the chain back into my pocket, closed my eyes and tried to picture myself safe at home.

It almost worked too. I was just drifting off when a clap of thunder, like the sound of the earth splitting apart, woke me. A moment later, it began to pour.

NINE

My first thought: Stay dry.
My second thought: *Water!*

I sat up and scrabbled for the metal bowl, and set it out to let it fill with water. I unscrewed the cap of the canteen and set it out too. But its mouth was so small that I knew it wouldn't collect much.

I sat huddled under the tree, watching the water hit the bottom of the bowl with so much force that it bounced right back up again. I held the sheet of plastic over my head like a little roof. It kept the top half of me dry, but the ground around me was packed hard, which meant it couldn't absorb all the rain that was coming down. Water ran in streams between the rocks and the exposed roots of trees. It wasn't long before the butt of my jeans was soaked through. I knew I had a decision to make. I could either look for some place to shelter during the storm, or I could give up trying to stay dry and take the opportunity to collect as much water as I could.

I thought about how thirsty I had been those first two days and about how far I might still have to walk. I also thought about the complete lack of water sources on my journey so far.

It didn't take long to make up my mind.

I jumped up and started to claw at the ground with my hands. I think I broke every one of my nails ripping at the hard-packed earth. Then I remembered the utensil set. I pulled it out of my jacket pocket and unsnapped the spoon and fork. I used them to gouge the earth. They weren't perfect—what I wouldn't have done for a shovel!—but they worked a lot better than my fingers. I dug with both hands. I dug as deep as I could, until finally I had a large hole about six inches deep. I lined it with the sheet of plastic and anchored the edges of the plastic with rocks.

The whole time, the rain hammered down.

I sat next to the hole, my knees pulled up to the chin, my arms wrapped around me, my head down, shivering all over. The temperature had dropped since I'd settled down to go to sleep. Or maybe it only felt that way because I was soaked to the skin. I started to worry again. What if I was coming down with something? Or what if all this cold and wet made me sick?

I told myself to stop saying those two words. I didn't need any more *what ifs* in my life. I needed water and food and shelter. I needed to get home.

The rain poured down. The hole filled and then overflowed. It got colder. I couldn't stop shivering. My teeth chattered. Thunder rolled and roared overhead. Lightning flashed across the inky black sky.

I heard a deafening sound, like an explosion, followed a few moments later by a crash, as if something had fallen out of the sky and plummeted to the earth. A tree, I thought. A tree had been struck by lightning, and from the sound of it, it wasn't far from where I was sitting. I gazed apprehensively at the pine tree that towered above me. I thought about those stories you hear from time to time about people getting caught outside during a lightning storm and taking shelter under a tree and then getting killed by lightning because lightning always strikes the tallest thing around. If you're under a tree that

gets hit by lightning, electricity goes into the earth
and kills you. I scrambled out from under the pine
tree and sat in the open. It was like sitting under a
waterfall, but I couldn't think what else to do. I put
my head down and rocked back and forth to try to
get warm. It didn't help. I closed my eyes and prayed
for sleep. It didn't come. The rain battered my head,
my shoulders, my back.

❦

The rain was still coming down at daybreak. But
even though the clouds overhead were thick and
gray, the forest gradually brightened a little. The sun
was up there somewhere, but it didn't look like the
rain was going to let up anytime soon.

I staggered to my feet. My body ached all over. My
clothes were so wet that they dripped. My sneakers
squelched with every step I took.

I drank as much water as I could hold from the
bowl and poured what was left into the canteen.
I filled the canteen the rest of the way to the top
with the water I had collected and screwed on the
cap. Then, carefully, I gathered the edges of the
plastic sheet and tied them together with the rope,

trapping the rest of the water inside. I set this plastic globe of water into the bowl. I would carry it with me and drink from it before starting on the canteen. Whatever else happened, I wouldn't have to worry about going thirsty for a while.

I gathered my few things, picked out two landmarks to guide me and set out into the dreary day.

The rain didn't let up. And I hadn't been imagining it; it really had gotten colder during the night. My breath plumed out in front of me.

I walked quickly, thinking it would help me warm up. But all it did was make me hungry. I stopped and peeled some bark from another birch tree. I chewed it while I trudged on.

Finally, late in the afternoon, the rain stopped. But the sun stayed hidden behind gray clouds.

I walked and walked, picking out landmark after landmark. I hoped I was going in the right direction, but with no sun visible in the sky, I had no way to check for sure.

I kept moving until it was almost dark. Before I settled for the night, I made an arrow out of twigs and pointed it in the direction I had been walking. I wished the sky would clear so that I could see the stars. If I could find the North Star, I could check that I had been walking in the right direction and hadn't veered off course. But the clouds hung on, obscuring the moon and stars.

I was exhausted from walking all day and shivering the entire night before. I hunkered down, pulled the rain-soaked blanket over my shoulders and tried to sleep. Pretty soon I found myself in the middle of a crazy kaleidoscope of a dream. There was my dad, alive and smiling as he rode his bike beside me down our street. Then my grandpa appeared on the other side of me, his long gray hair flying out behind him, even though in real life I had never seen my grandpa on a bicycle. Suddenly they vanished, as if someone had switched them off, and I was walking down a long dark corridor. Light seeped out around the edges of a door up ahead. Someone was laughing. I approached the door cautiously and pushed it open.

My mom was sitting on a red velvet sofa in front of a fireplace. She was laughing merrily at something, but I couldn't see what it was. I walked toward her. As I got closer, I saw that there was someone with her. A man. My mom turned to look at me. She was smiling radiantly. I had never seen her look so happy. Then man turned too, and I saw that it was Gregg. Like my mom, he was smiling. But both their smiles faded when they saw me. Suddenly they weren't happy anymore.

I woke with a jolt, but nothing felt real. Instead of shivering, I was hot all over. The forest floor was thick with mist. From somewhere inside it, I heard the snap and pop of fallen twigs and branches being crushed underfoot. But under the foot of what— or who?

A face broke through the mist. It was my father. Blood was running down his face, but he smiled and beckoned to me. I got up and followed him home.

TEN

I woke up the next morning exactly where I had fallen asleep. The sky was gray, but the rain had stopped. My clothes were still soaked through, and I was shaking, but now, instead of being cold, I was burning up. I closed my eyes and went back to sleep.

When I awoke the second time, the sun was high in the sky. I drank from the canteen, refilled it with the water in the plastic bubble, packed everything up and staggered to my feet. My head spun, when I bent down to pick up a stick and plant it in the ground, and throbbed as I went through the process of orienting myself. When I finally set off into the west, every joint in my body ached.

What was wrong with me? I stumbled with every step I took. My feet felt like granite boulders. I tripped over a tree root, a rock, another tree root. No matter how much water I drank, I was still thirsty. It felt like someone was pounding on my temples with a hammer.

I walked, I stumbled, I tripped—until finally I couldn't make myself take another step. I sank to the ground. I was sick, and that scared me. Was it from being wet and cold for so long? Was it from drinking bad water? Had I poisoned myself? Was it from all the birch bark I had eaten? I forced myself back to my feet. I had to keep moving. I just had to. If I was sick, that made it all the more critical for me to get to my destination as soon as possible. I couldn't let anything slow me down.

I stumbled on for what seemed like an hour but was probably more like a few minutes. The next time I tripped and fell, I didn't get up. Instead I curled up on the ground and closed my eyes.

When I opened them again, it was pitch dark, and I could see the stars overhead.

I cursed myself.

I had wasted most of a day sleeping. I would never get home. I was shivering uncontrollably.

My forehead was as hot as a burning coal. What if I couldn't move when the sun came up? What would I do then?

I felt like crying. But instead I got angry with myself. Crying didn't do any good. All those tears after my father died had proved that to me. Crying didn't make me feel better. It didn't change anything. And it sure wouldn't get me home.

Grandpa had told me that any situation usually comes down to two choices. He said they were usually the same two choices.

My situation was that I was lost in the woods and desperately wanted to get home. But I was sick and tired—and discouraged.

The two choices I had were to either curl up into a little ball and cry and hope that someone would eventually rescue me, or, I could get a grip on myself and accept that it was all up to me. The only person I could rely on to get me home was me. That meant I had to keep my wits about me. I had to keep going. I had to refuse to give up.

I also had to accept that at that exact moment there was nothing I could do. I had to wait for the sun to rise again.

Well, almost nothing.

The stars were out. Since I had been too tired and too sick to mark my direction with an arrow before I went to sleep, I could use the stars now to take a reading and to double-check my direction in the morning.

I searched the sky until I found the Big Dipper. I focused on the two stars that made up the end of the dipper and followed them across the sky to the brightest star there was—the North Star. "If you walk toward the North Star," Grandpa said, "you'll always be walking north." I dug the knife out of my pocket and scored an arrow in the ground. I felt a little better. I settled back and waited for the sun to rise.

The next time I opened my eyes, the sun was high above the treetops. I still felt sore and feverish, but my headache had faded and I was hungry and thirsty again. I opened the canteen and sniffed the water. Was it making me sick? Should I throw it out? Then what would I do? Thirst won out in the end. I drank deeply and refilled the canteen with the remaining water from the plastic bubble. I stepped unsteadily out into the sun of a little clearing up ahead.

My clothes were still damp, but they were no longer soaked through.

I used a stick and my watch to recalculate where west was and checked the direction against the north-pointing arrow I had made in the ground the night before. I was relieved to find that I hadn't veered off course. I set out into the morning.

My stomach growled. I was so hungry that I felt weak. But there wasn't a single birch tree in sight. Instead I was surrounded by pine trees and, up ahead, a stand of cedars. Maybe that would change. I kept walking.

Pine.

Pine.

Pine.

Cedar.

Pine.

The sun began to sink again.

I had to eat something—anything.

A rotting log blocked my path. I stared at it.

Grandpa and I had come across plenty of rotting logs on our hikes. Once Grandpa had broken one open to show me what was inside. It was filled with fat, squirming, worm-like creatures, writhing all over each other in a heap. Grubs, Grandpa said. He picked

93

up one of the squirming creatures and popped it into his mouth. I watched in astonishment as he swallowed it, grinned and rubbed his belly contentedly.

"I know they don't look appetizing," he said.

Appetizing?

"They look disgusting. If you're trying to gross me out, Grandpa, you're doing a great job."

"They taste better than they look."

"That's not saying much."

Grandpa laughed. "They're also rich in protein," he said. "When I was a couple of years younger than you are now, I decided to show my father how grown up I was. While he made one of his treks into town, I went out hunting on my own. I thought I'd surprise him with some rabbits or maybe even a deer when he came back. It didn't work out that way though. I got myself good and lost. Worse, I managed to drop my rifle over the edge of a ravine. Pretty soon I had no choice—it was either eat grubs or starve. So I ate grubs. They saved my life."

"I'd rather starve," I said. I'd meant it too.

But that was when I with my grandpa and we had a small camp stove with us so that soon after that we were eating stew and washing it down with hot tea. Now I was on my own with no stove, no tea and nothing to make stew out of. Apart from strips of birch bark, I hadn't eaten anything in days. And I had no idea how much longer I might have to walk.

I stared at the log in front of me and wondered what was inside. I stepped up to it, wrapped my fingers around one rough end and pulled as hard as I could. The log was soft and spongy. It came apart easily in my hands, exposing the inside. Sure enough, it was squirming with fat disgusting grubs. Just looking at them made me queasy. I swallowed hard before reaching out with one hand—oh my god, they were so gross!—and plucking one fat grub from the seething mass. It twisted and wriggled its soft white body, and I almost dropped it in disgust. There was no way I was going to be able to put something that alive and that revolting into my mouth. I remembered what I had told Grandpa: *I'd rather starve.*

Now I'd rather not starve.

I squeezed my eyes closed, tipped my head back and dropped the grub into my mouth. I had to fight the urge to spit it out again. I felt it writhe on the back of my tongue. I tried to swallow it, and gagged. Finally, my face twisted in revulsion, I choked it down.

Yuck!

For a moment, I was sure I was going to throw up. That was the most disgusting thing I had ever done. The fat little bug was probably writhing down in my stomach. I looked down at the log again. I didn't doubt what Grandpa had told me. I didn't doubt that the grubs were rich in protein or that they had saved his life. But I wished that it would only take one to satisfy my hunger. That way, I wouldn't have to eat any more of them.

Slowly I bent down and plucked another one from the revolting little colony. It was fatter and squirmier than the first one. I closed my eyes again, popped it into my mouth, bit down quickly, tried not to think about the goo that suddenly ran down the back of my throat, and forced myself to swallow. The second one didn't go down any more easily than the first.

I picked up another grub. Then another and another. Every single one filled me with revulsion. Every single one made me want to throw up. But I ate them anyway. I wanted to go home, and if eating grubs was what it was going to take, then I would do what my grandpa had done—I would eat grubs.

Finally, astonishingly, my stomach felt full. For the first time since I had found myself in that miserable little shack, it wasn't grumbling and groaning from hunger.

I started walking again and kept going as the sun continued to sink. I was feeling so good for a change that I decided to keep walking until it was too dark to see. It seemed like a great idea—until I stepped onto something black that I thought was a rock.

I was wrong.

 ELEVEN

The black thing that I'd seen wasn't a rock. It was a hole. My foot plunged into it, throwing me off balance. My upper body lurched forward as my foot went down. Pain ripped through my right ankle and burned up my leg. I screamed. I had never felt anything that even came close to the searing agony I was experiencing. And it didn't let up. *Oh my god, oh my god, oh my god.*

I lay motionless for a few moments, stunned by the pain. Then, slowly, I tried to move myself into a sitting position. Tears streamed down my cheeks. Once I had eased my butt down onto the ground, I grabbed my right knee and gently pulled my foot out of the hole. Blinding pain shot through my ankle.

I was sure that when I got my foot out of that hole, there would be blood everywhere.

There wasn't. There was no blood at all.

But the pain made me cry out again. I sat there for a few moments, hoping it would subside.

It didn't.

I felt a wave of panic wash over me. What if…?

Get up, Steph. You have to get up. You have to try to walk. You have to get out of here.

I drew in a deep breath. I planted my hands firmly on the ground and got my good foot under me. Even that small movement jarred my ankle and sent a shock of agony through me. I steadied myself on one foot and looked around. There was a tree close by. I dragged myself over to it and grabbed hold of the trunk. Slowly I eased myself to a standing position. I was breathing hard. My underarms prickled with sweat.

Okay, I told myself. *So far, so good*—as long as I ignored the feeling that someone had thrust a white-hot sword through my ankle and was twisting it this way and that.

I put a little weight on my right foot—and almost collapsed from the pain.

You can't stay here, Steph, I told myself. *You have to keep moving.*

I scanned the immediate area for something to use as a walking stick. A massive tree branch lay on the forest floor to my left, like a giant's discarded fan. I made my way gingerly to it on one foot, holding on to whatever I could for support. One sturdy branch had been partially snapped off by the fall. I wrestled with it until it broke off completely, and I tested my weight on it. It would have to do. I leaned heavily on it and tried to take a step.

I collapsed again. I couldn't do it. It was too hard, too painful.

You have two choices, Steph. Always the same two choices.

Give up or go on.

I grasped the walking stick and maneuvered myself back up onto my good foot. This time I put all my weight on the stick and swung my hurt ankle forward without touching the ground. Even that small movement made me want to scream, but I managed to stay upright.

My progress was painfully slow—with a heavy emphasis on painful. I put as much of my weight as I could on the branch—my walking stick—but every step sent a searing shock up my leg. Whenever I came to a fallen tree, which happened with discouraging regularity, I had to sit down on the trunk, swing one foot, followed by the other, and struggle to a standing position again. Twice I put my walking stick on a rock only to have it slip off when I leaned on it, sending me crashing to the ground. Twice I cried out with pain.

I hadn't gone far before I had to stop and rest. I curled up under a tree, wrapped myself in my ratty old blanket and wept. I knew it wouldn't help, but my ankle hurt so much. I was hungry again, and thirsty. I was cold. I was sick. And now I could barely walk. I was never going to get home. I was going to be stuck in these woods until I died.

I slept fitfully that night. Every time I moved, pain shot up my leg. When morning came, I was as exhausted as if I had run a marathon, and I was still feverish. I sat under the tree, feeling sorry for myself. Why couldn't someone come along and find me? Why couldn't I get lucky just for once?

But no one came along.

I dug my walking stick into the ground and slowly pulled myself up. I put some weight on my injured foot to see if it had gotten better overnight.

It hadn't.

I wanted to lie down again. Maybe if I rested for a day, the pain would go away.

Or maybe it wouldn't. Maybe I would just end up wasting another day—a day without food or water.

I set off again.

I told myself that things couldn't get worse.

About an hour later, I emerged from the woods into a clearing and found myself staring at a black bear. The bear stared back at me. It was full-grown but scrawny, which told me that it must have recently come out of hibernation. That meant it was probably hungry.

Everything went silent around me. Everything disappeared except the bear. It was as if I was at one end of a dark tunnel and the only thing I could see against the light at the other end was that bear.

I told myself: *Don't panic.*

I told myself: *Don't look directly at it.*

I told myself: *Don't run.*

I told myself: *Don't turn your back on it. In fact, don't turn at all.*

Grandpa had taught me all about bears.

He said that bear attacks were rare. He said they happened when a bear saw a human as a threat or—I swallowed hard as I remembered this—when the bear was predatory. A bear that was predatory regarded humans as a source of food.

I told myself that this bear was probably not predatory. I told myself that I had surprised it, that's all. Slowly, awkwardly, I took a step backward, away from the bear. If I could fade into the woods, maybe it wouldn't feel threatened. Maybe it would forget all about me. Maybe it would go away.

I backed up another step, keeping my eyes on the ground. It had been hard enough moving forward with my injured ankle and walking stick. Going backward was even trickier. With my head still bowed, I peeked at the clearing. The bear was still standing there. It was still watching me.

I eased my walking stick behind me again, feeling for a place to put it down. This time, when I tried to step back, I stumbled and fell. I couldn't help myself—I let out a yelp as I crashed to the ground.

I heard a loud huffing sound. Oh my god! The bear reared up onto its hind legs. I had startled it, and it didn't like that. It looked enormous and fierce.

I reached for my walking stick and began to struggle to my one good foot.

That's when I heard another sound behind me—a loud clap, like another large animal snapping a dry branch underfoot. Was there another bear behind me? Worse, were there bear cubs behind me? Had I come between a mother bear and her babies? A mother bear would do anything to protect her offspring. She would even attack.

I was breathing hard. I scrambled to my feet, wrenching my ankle again. I had to bite my lip to stop from crying out. All I wanted was to get out of the bear's way.

The bear thumped down onto all fours and charged across the clearing toward me. I opened my mouth to scream, but no sound came out. All I could see, all I could think about, was that bear barreling toward me. I knew that running wouldn't do any good. Grandpa said it was impossible to outrun a bear. But terror gripped me. I had to do something, and running was the only thing I could think of—injured ankle or not.

I hadn't taken more than two steps when my ankle collapsed under me and I fell.

I lay face down on the ground and spread my legs to make it harder for the bear to flip me over.

I intertwined my hands over the back of my neck to protect myself. I told myself that my only chance was to play dead. I squeezed my eyes shut. Every muscle in my body tensed as I waited for the bear to fall on top of me. I tried not to think of its sharp teeth and sharper claws.

TWELVE

*B*ang!
Bang! Bang!

Three explosions, like gunshots.

A crash.

Silence.

I was still breathing. There was no bear on top of me.

I opened my eyes and raised my head.

A man was standing a few feet away from me. He was tall and gaunt, with a scruffy beard and scruffier hair. He was wearing faded jeans, scarred boots and a red-and-black flannel shirt under what looked like an army jacket. He was holding a rifle. I twisted around and saw the bear lying on the ground behind me. I started to shake all over. I had been terrified of the bear, but I was even more terrified of the man. Where had he come from? Had he been following me?

Was he the man who had taken me?

He went directly to the bear, still aiming his rifle at it, and nudged it with one foot. When the bear didn't move, he stepped a little closer. He stood there for a minute, staring at the bear, before finally lowering his rifle and turning back to me.

"Get up," he said roughly.

He didn't ask my name. He didn't ask what I was doing there. It was as if he already knew. I felt sick all over, from dread this time, not panic. It *was* him. It was the man who had drugged me and brought me out into the middle of nowhere. I couldn't make myself move. I was paralyzed with fear.

"You heard me," the man said. "Get up." He started toward me.

This was it. This was the end. He'd tracked me and found me.

"Please," I whimpered. I wanted to be brave, but all I could think was that he was going to do to me what he had done to that first girl, the one they had found dead. "Please don't kill me. Please."

The man stopped. He looked at me. Then he looked at his rifle.

"Kill you?" he said. "Why on earth would I kill you?" He sounded genuinely surprised.

I couldn't stop blubbering.

He seemed flustered by my tears. He came over to me slowly, like I was a baby deer and he was afraid to spook me. He reached down with one hand.

"Come on now," he said. His voice was soft now instead of gruff. "Get up. I'm not going to hurt you— even though, if you ask me, you should have more sense than to be out here in the first place."

I couldn't have moved even if I'd wanted to, and I didn't want to. He was pretending to care. It was all a cruel trick. He was probably insane. You had to be insane to be a serial killer.

His hand closed around my wrist. It was rough and calloused.

"Please," I moaned.

"For the love of Pete, I'm not going to hurt you," he said, gruff again. He set his rifle aside and pulled me to my feet. I winced and groaned when I accidentally put too much weight on my bad foot.

"What's the matter?" he said.

I couldn't answer.

He looked down at my foot. He told me to lean on him. I didn't want to touch him. He told me again. When I still didn't obey, he scooped me up, carried me to a rock and plunked me down on it. He pushed up the leg of my jeans and worked off my sneaker. Pain washed over me in waves. I was sure I was going to throw up. He ran his rough hands over my ankle. I cried out.

"There now," he said. "I'm just checking. It's not broken, but it looks like you wrenched it pretty bad." He looked me over, taking in my filthy clothes, my dirty face and my wild tangled hair. "How long have you been out here?"

I stared at him.

He repeated his question.

Instead of answering, I said, "What are you going to do to me?"

"Do to you? I'm going to see that you get back where you belong, that's what."

"You're not going to...to kill me?"

"No," he said, "I'm not going to kill you." There was something about the way he looked right into my eyes that made me believe him. He wasn't the one. When he asked me again how long I had been in the woods, I told him.

"What in the name of Pete are you doing out here all by yourself?" he said.

"Trying to get home."

He shook his head impatiently.

"What I mean is, what brought you here in the first place?"

"Somebody kidnapped me."

"Kidnapped you?" He squinted at me. "Where'd you say you were from?"

I told him. He studied me for a moment, and I saw a flicker of understanding in his eyes. He turned his back to me and squatted down.

"Hop on," he said.

"No, it's okay."

He looked over his shoulder at me.

"You can't walk on that ankle, and I don't have one of those damned cell phones everyone seems to be carrying these days. Les Andruksen's place isn't far. Hop on and I'll carry you."

Reluctantly, I climbed onto his back. I hadn't had a piggyback ride since I was a little girl, and it felt weird to be carried by someone I didn't know. He scooped up his rifle and set off as if I were no heavier than a bedroll. He'd said our destination wasn't far, but he hiked along for over an hour without slowing.

Finally I heard something. It sounded like…a car, whizzing down a highway. A few minutes later, we left the trees behind us and stepped out into a roadside clearance. Beyond it lay a paved two-lane road, flanked on both sides by deep ditches. The man took his time going down into the ditch and then climbing up the other side, with me still riding his back. We crossed the road, and he started the long hike up a graveled driveway to a house set on a rise well back from the road. There was a barn behind it and fields all around. A herd of cows chewed contentedly in a grassy pasture.

He carried me up onto the porch and helped me slide off his back. He pressed the doorbell.

A woman answered.

"Zeke!" she said. "What a surprise. Come in. Can I get you some coffee?" Then she noticed me.

"Is Les here?" Zeke said.

"He's out back. Come in, and I'll call him."

Zeke helped me inside and sat me down on a bench in the front hall. The woman was back a few moments later. A man followed her. He was wearing denim coveralls and heavy boots that he probably should have taken off at the back door. He looked at me, frowning, as if something was bothering him. He turned to Zeke and said, "Is everything okay?"

"I was out looking for that bear," he said.

Les nodded, as if he knew exactly which bear Zeke was talking about.

"I found him," Zeke said. "He was charging this girl."

"Charging her?" Les said.

"Yup. But I took care of him."

Les stared at me again with that same frown on his face.

"What's your name?"

"Stephanie Rawls."

His expression changed, as if that cleared up whatever had been bothering him.

"You're that girl who's been missing," he said.

I nodded.

"I'm Les Andruksen. This is my wife Susan. I'm a police officer in Angel Falls."

Angel Falls? That was a long way from home.

"Your mom has been worried sick about you," he said. "Are you hurt?"

"She's wrenched her ankle," Zeke said. "It's swelled up like a cantaloupe, but as far as I can tell, it's not broken."

"When was the last time you ate anything?" Mr. Andruksen said.

"I'm not sure. A few days ago."

"Susan, heat up some soup," he said. He turned to me. "I bet you're hungry."

Was I ever!

"We'll get some hot soup into you, and then I'll run you up to the hospital to get you checked out."

"I'll find her some clean clothes," Mrs. Andruksen said. "We should let her wash up."

Mr. Andruksen shook his head. "I need to talk to Stephanie first," he said. "She can wash up later. Right now she should eat something." He glanced at Zeke. "I'd appreciate it if you could stick around for a little while, Zeke. I may need you. Susan will get you some coffee."

Zeke nodded. He followed Mrs. Andruksen down the hall to the back of the house. Mr. Andruksen helped me into the dining room and pulled out a chair for me.

"What happened, Stephanie?" he said. "Where have you been for the past week?"

"I was on my way home from the bus when someone grabbed me from behind. The next thing I knew, I woke up in a shack in the middle of the woods."

Mr. Andruksen frowned. "Someone grabbed you?"

"Yes. I was taking a shortcut through a field near my house. I know it was a dumb thing to do. I wish I hadn't done it." I was close to tears again. I struggled to control myself. "Someone grabbed me. I think he jabbed me with a needle. He must have drugged me, because when I woke up, I was tied up in a shack."

He nodded, but I didn't see the sympathy in his eyes that I had been expecting.

"Then what happened?"

"I managed to untie myself, and I got away from there as fast as I could. I've been walking ever since."

He sat very still. Only his eyes moved. He studied me methodically, as if he were trying to memorize every detail of my appearance.

"What about whoever you say grabbed you and jabbed you with a needle?" he said finally. "Where was that person while you were escaping?"

"I don't know. I never saw him."

"What do you mean, you never saw him? Was he wearing a mask?"

A mask? Was that important? Was the man who had taken those other two girls wearing a mask?

"No," I said. "At least, I don't think so. He grabbed me from behind, so I didn't see him. Then he drugged me. When I woke up, I was alone in a shack in the woods somewhere."

"Alone? The person you say grabbed you wasn't there?"

I shook my head. "But I was afraid he would come back." I started to shake uncontrollably. "I was afraid he would see that I was trying to escape, and then he would do something awful to me. But he never came back."

"You keep saying *he*. If you didn't see him, how do you know for sure it was a man?"

"Well...I guess I don't," I admitted. "But he seemed strong, so I'm just assuming."

He leaned back in his chair.

"So you were on your way home...from where?"

I told him.

"And someone you didn't see grabbed you and drugged you and took you to a shack. But you didn't see him when he grabbed you, and you didn't see him at the shack either? Is that right?"

"That's right. And I was so scared he would come back. I knew I had to get out of there."

"How did you manage to escape? What exactly did you do?"

I told him. He frowned.

"He tied you up with rope?" he said.

I nodded.

His eyes went to my wrists, but he didn't say anything.

"How long do you think you were in that shack before you escaped?"

"I'm not sure." I had no idea what day it was. I had to ask.

"It's Friday," he said.

Friday? I tried to count the days since I had woken up. If it was Friday, then I must have been in that cabin for more than one day.

"It was Saturday when he grabbed me," I said. "I thought it was the next day when I woke up, but if this is Friday, then I must have woken up on Monday." It didn't seem possible. What on earth had he drugged me with?

"Did you notice anything different when you woke up, Stephanie?"

Different? Hadn't he been listening to me?

"I was tied up," I said, my voice shrill now. I didn't understand what was going on. Why was he asking me such strange questions? "I had no idea where I was, and I was tied up."

"It's okay, Stephanie," he said, his voice soft and soothing. "I'm just trying to get a picture in my mind of what happened. That's my job. Okay?"

"Okay."

"What I meant when I asked you if you noticed anything different was…well, for example, did you notice if all your clothes were the same or if anything had been, well, disturbed?"

Disturbed? Oh my god.

"Everything seemed the same," I said. "I was tied up, that's all."

"Did you see anything that made you think that the person who took you had been in the shack with you while you were unconscious?"

What did he mean? "Like what?"

"Like, say, blankets or a pillow or anything that he might have slept on? Or any belongings of his— maybe a backpack or duffle bag, something like that? Or food?"

"There wasn't any food in the shack. I looked. There was nothing like that."

"Okay, well, then maybe the smell of food. If he'd cooked anything…"

"There was no smell of food." I was one hundred percent sure that I would have noticed. "It looked like no one had been there in years. The place was covered with cobwebs."

He nodded thoughtfully.

"Do you think you could show me where this shack is, Stephanie?"

"I…I don't know. I don't think so." I hated to say that because of the way he was looking at me. "It was nighttime when I got free. I looked around as best as I could. I didn't see any roads or even tire tracks. All I know is that ever since I got free, I've been walking west."

He perked up at that.

"Why west?"

"Because I could see the glow of lights from the top of a hill near the shack."

"How did you know it was west from where you were? Did you have a compass?"

I shook my head. "But I know how to find my direction." I explained it to him, adding, "My grandpa taught me. My grandpa knew everything about living in the woods." I told him about wilderness spaghetti.

"It's lucky that you know as much about wilderness survival as you do, Stephanie," he said. "I didn't see anything like that mentioned in the report your mother made to the police."

"She didn't know," I said. She had been so involved with her new life when I got back from Grandpa's that she hadn't asked very much about how I had spent my summer. And I was so mad at her that I didn't volunteer the information.

"Is there anything else you can tell me, Stephanie? Anything at all?"

That's when I remembered the chain. I dug into my pocket and pulled it out.

"I found this caught on the lining of my jacket," I said. "It's not mine. I never saw it before. And I know it wasn't there when I got on the bus to come home. I'm pretty sure I pulled it off whoever grabbed me." I described to him what I remembered happening.

Mr. Andruksen looked at the broken chain. I couldn't tell what he was thinking. He got up, found a piece of paper and asked me to put the chain on it. He folded the paper around it like an envelope and excused himself. I heard him speaking to someone out in the front hall, but I couldn't make out what he was saying. I heard the front door open and close. Mr. Andruksen came back into the dining room from the front hall. Mrs. Andruksen came in from the kitchen. She was carrying a bowl of steaming soup, which she set in front of me. It smelled heavenly.

"Eat up, Stephanie," Mr. Andruksen said. "Then we'll get your ankle looked at."

"Can I call my mom?"

"I'll take care of that too," he said. "Susan, stay with her, will you? I have to make a few calls."

The soup tasted even better than it smelled. I devoured the whole bowl without stopping and eagerly said yes when Mrs. Andruksen offered me seconds.

THIRTEEN

First we went to the hospital, where they x-rayed my ankle. It turned out Zeke was right. It wasn't broken. But it was badly sprained. After the doctor examined me, he had a nurse wrap a big elastic bandage around it.

"I don't want you to put any weight on it for at least a week," he said. "Then we'll take another look."

The nurse brought me some crutches.

While I was in the hospital, another police officer arrived—a woman. She brought me some clean clothes and asked me if I needed any help changing. I said no. She told me to put my old clothes on the end of the bed and said that she would come to collect them. Before she left the room, she scraped the dirt from under my fingernails. She also looked carefully at my arm where I had been jabbed with the needle.

After I had changed into the clean clothes, Mr.— I mean, Sergeant—Andruksen came back into the room.

"I called your mother," he said. "She and her fiancé are on their way to the police station."

Fiancé? Since when had my mom started referring to Gregg as her fiancé?

I didn't see Mom and Gregg when I hobbled into the police station with Sergeant Andruksen. They probably hadn't arrived yet. It was a long drive from our place up to Angel Falls.

Sergeant Andruksen showed me into an interview room. He asked me if I was hungry.

"Starving," I said, just as another man came into the room. He was wearing a dark suit.

"Stephanie, this is Detective Carlysle," Sergeant Andruksen said. "He's going to ask you some questions about what happened. I'll see if I can get you something to eat."

He disappeared. Detective Carlysle asked me to sit down. He asked if I needed any help.

"I can manage," I said. I hobbled over to the table and eased myself down onto a chair. Detective Carlysle sat down across from me.

"Tell me everything you can remember about what happened, Stephanie."

"I already told Sergeant Andruksen."

"I know. And I appreciate that. But I need you to tell me too. Do you think you can do that?"

I nodded. I told Detective Carlysle the same thing I had told Sergeant Andruksen. He listened intently and didn't interrupt me even once. As soon as I finished telling my story for the second time, Sergeant Andruksen came into the room. I could be wrong, but I had the feeling that he had been out there watching and waiting for me to finish before he came back in. He had a packaged sandwich and a bottle of juice with him.

"I hope tuna is okay," he said.

"It's fine. Thanks."

Detective Carlysle stood up.

"I have to talk to Sergeant Andruksen for a few minutes, Stephanie," he said. "I'll be right back."

As soon as they left, I ripped the plastic wrap off

the sandwich and took a huge bite. It was the best tuna sandwich I had ever tasted. I devoured it even faster than I had devoured Mrs. Andruksen's soup, and I washed it down with the bottle of juice.

❧

"Is my mom here yet?" I asked when Detective Carlysle returned fifteen minutes later.

"We're talking to her right now."

"When can I see her?"

"Soon." He sat down across the table from me again. "How do you and your mom get along, Stephanie?"

"Okay, I guess." I wished I could see her right away. I'd never missed her as much as I had when I was out there in those woods. I wanted to hug her. I wanted to apologize to her for every mean thing I had ever said. I wanted to tell her that I loved her.

"I understand it was pretty rough on you when your father died," Detective Carlysle said.

"It was rough on both of us."

"I'm sure it was. It's been pretty rough since then too, hasn't it?"

"What do you mean?"

"Your mother told us that you and your dad were very close. She said you took it hard when she started seeing someone else. She said you were angry with her because you thought she didn't love your father."

"Well, yes, sort of, I guess," I said. What did that have to do with anything? I wasn't angry at her now. "I want to see my mom. I want to go home."

"I'm sure you do. But I need you to answer a few more questions first, okay?"

I was tired of answering questions, but if that was what it was going to take. "Okay."

"Have you ever run away from home, Stephanie?"

"What?" Why was he asking me that?

"Your mother told us—she told the police when she reported you missing—that since your father died, you've run away several times. She said it always happens after you and she have an argument. Is that right?"

"Yes," I said. "But that's not what happened this time. Somebody grabbed me. Somebody drugged me."

"I understand you had a big argument with your mother a couple of days before you disappeared," he said.

"Yes, but—"

"It was about your mother's fiancé, wasn't it?"

There was that word again—*fiancé*.

"Yes," I said. "But—"

"I understand you argued with your mother a lot about her fiancé."

I just stared at him.

"It must be hard," he said. "I heard what happened to your father. I bet it's hard to think about anyone else taking his place."

"No one will ever take his place!" I said. How dare he even suggest such a thing! "My father was really smart and funny and—" I shook my head. "Gregg isn't anything like that. I don't understand what my mom sees in him."

"Is that why you ran away all those times?"

I didn't want to talk about it, but I knew I had to answer him.

"I guess," I said.

"Did you run away last Saturday night, Stephanie? Did you want to punish your mother after the fight you had with her? Did you want to teach her a lesson?"

"*What*? No! I told you what happened. Someone grabbed me. You must know about those other two girls who disappeared. They were the same age as me.

126

They had long brown hair, just like me. They were kidnapped when they were on their way home after dark—just like me."

"Is that what gave you the idea, Stephanie? You wanted your mother to think you'd been kidnapped too?"

"I *was* kidnapped!" Wasn't he listening to me? "I was drugged and I was kidnapped—by the same guy who took those other two girls." I realized I hadn't heard any news for a week. "Did they ever find that second girl?"

He nodded grimly. I didn't have to ask whether she'd been alive or not.

"You know a lot about those girls, don't you, Stephanie?" he said. "There's a newspaper article on your fridge door. You knew that everyone, including your mother, has been on edge about them. You've run away after arguments with your mother before."

"Yes. But I didn't run away this time."

"Are you sure, Stephanie?"

"Of course I'm sure! Do you think I would make this up?" What was the matter with him? Then I got it. I understood. "You don't believe me. You don't believe I was kidnapped."

"I didn't say that."

But I knew I was right.

"You would have been happier if you'd found me dead and clutching that chain," I said. "Then you'd be sure you had some kind of clue to help you catch the guy who killed those other two girls. But I'm not dead. I'm alive. I escaped. And you're so disappointed that you're accusing me of lying."

"I'm not accusing you of anything, Stephanie. I'm just trying to make sense out of what you said and what we know about the other two girls. That's my job." He stood up. "Do you want to see your mother?"

I nodded. He walked to the door and opened it. A moment later, my mom rushed into the room and threw her arms around me as I was struggling to my feet. She hugged me so hard that I thought she was going to squeeze all the air out of me. When she finally stepped back to take a good look at me, tears were running down her cheeks. Her face was pale, and there were dark circles under her eyes. I had been scared the whole time I was out in the woods, and I'd known—at least, I'd hoped—that my mom had been worried about me. Now I saw that she had been more worried than I had imagined.

"You look so thin and tired," she said. "And your

ankle…" She hugged me again, even harder this time. "I was so worried. People kept saying that it was probably that serial killer. I…I can't believe I'm saying this, but I was hoping that you'd just run away. I love you, Stephanie. I don't know what I would do if anything ever happened to you."

"I love you too, Mom." I was crying too. "I thought I was never going to get home. I thought I was going to—"

"Shhh!" she said. She hugged me again and held me for a long time. It felt good. For the first time in a week, I felt safe. "Come on," she said finally. "Let's get you home and cleaned up." She kept her arm around me while I hobbled out of the room on crutches.

Gregg was outside talking to Sergeant Andruksen. He looked as pale and exhausted as my mom, but his face lit up when he saw me.

"We were so worried," he said, coming toward me as if he was going to throw his arms around me. Suddenly he stopped, embarrassed. His arms hung awkwardly at his sides. I couldn't blame him. The old me would have screamed if he'd tried to hug me. How was he supposed to know that I had changed? "We were afraid we might never see you again, Steph."

"I was afraid I'd never see you again either," I said. "I'm sorry I've been such a pain, Gregg."

My mom squeezed my shoulder. She was smiling through her tears now.

"You're not a pain," Gregg said. "You're just a kid who misses her dad, that's all." He glanced at Sergeant Andruksen. "We're good to go, right? We can take her home?"

Sergeant Andruksen looked at Detective Carlysle, who nodded.

"If you think of anything else you want to tell me, Stephanie," he said, "anything at all, call me." He gave me his card.

I looked at Detective Carlysle. I didn't like the things he'd been asking me.

"Can I ask you a question?" I said to Sergeant Andruksen. "In private?"

He looked surprised, but he nodded and walked me down the hall away from Detective Carlysle, my mom and Gregg.

"What's up, Stephanie?"

"He doesn't believe me," I said, nodding at Detective Carlysle.

"He's a detective, Stephanie. He doesn't make up his mind about anything until he has all the facts, and we're still working on gathering them."

"What about the chain I gave you? Won't that help?"

"We're going to look into it. I can promise you that. If there's any way that chain can help us find whoever took you, we'll find it. And, Stephanie? Don't mention the chain to anyone, okay? There are always details that we don't make public. It can give us an advantage, you understand?"

I nodded.

I wanted to ask him one last question. I wanted to ask if *he* believed me. But I was afraid what his answer might be.

FOURTEEN

The whole way home, my mom kept turning around to look at me in the backseat, as if she were afraid that I would disappear again at any moment. Every so often she said, "I was so worried. I kept thinking, what if I never see my baby again? What if…?"

Gregg squeezed her hand.

"She's right here with us, Trish," he said. "It's okay now. She's safe."

My mom turned and looked at me again, her eyes glistening with tears. I knew exactly how she felt. I felt the same way myself, only in reverse. She was glad to have me back; I was glad to be back.

The first thing I did when I got home was take a shower. I couldn't believe how filthy I was. When I looked in the mirror in the bathroom, I saw that the pores on my face were clogged with dirt. I stood under the hot water forever and ever, soaping myself over and over again. Finally I washed my hair, dried myself off and pulled on some clean sweats.

The house was filled with the most incredible aroma. I recognized it instantly. My mom was making lasagna.

"It'll be ready in an hour," she said. "If you can't wait, I can make you something to tide you over."

"I can wait." My mom made the best lasagna I had ever tasted. She had gotten the recipe from her grandmother, whose mother had brought it with her from the old country. My mom's lasagna was always worth waiting for.

Gregg was in the family room when I came downstairs. The family room is next to the kitchen, but two steps down. There's no wall between the two rooms, which Gregg likes. It means he can watch TV from the kitchen table while he eats. He stood up and smiled at me when I went into the kitchen, but he stayed where he was. For once he seemed to understand that I needed to be with my mom.

My mom made me hot chocolate, and I sat at the table and watched her while she made a salad and some homemade salad dressing.

"That police sergeant told us what happened," she said. "He said you did an amazing job of handling yourself in the woods. He said your grandfather taught you how to do that. You never told me about that."

"Things were hard when I got back from Grandpa's," I said.

My mom started to tear up again. "When I think of all the mean things I said about Charlie…" Charlie was my grandpa's name. "I wish I'd known. I wish you'd told me."

"You had other things on your mind, Mom. And anyway, I don't think Grandpa cared what anyone thought about him. He was happy doing what he was doing."

⁂

The three of us—Mom and Gregg and me—had supper together. I finished one helping of lasagna and held out my plate so that my mom could give me more.

"That cop that called us, he said you weren't able to tell them anything about the guy that grabbed you," Gregg said. "How come? Was he wearing a mask or something?"

"Gregg," my mom said softly, shaking her head. She glanced at me as if she was afraid the question had upset me.

"It's okay, Mom. I don't mind." I looked across the table at Gregg. "I don't know if he was wearing a mask. I never saw him. He grabbed me from behind and drugged me."

"But when you woke up, you must have seen him—at least how tall he was, whether he was fat or thin, young or old, something like that. You heard what the cops said, Steph. Anything at all you can tell them will help."

"I don't know anything. I didn't see anything." I turned to my mom. "There was this detective who asked me a lot of questions. I don't think he believed me. I think he thought I was making it up."

"Making it up?" My mom was stunned. "That nice police sergeant I spoke to never said anything about making things up."

"The detective kept asking me if I'd run away before."

"Surely they don't think—," my mom began. She looked at Gregg in dismay.

Gregg was silent for a moment. He took a bite of lasagna and seemed to chew it forever. "That's not what happened, right, Steph?" he said finally. "You didn't run away, did you?"

"No!" I tried to stand up, I was so angry. Pain shot up my leg, reminding me of my sprained ankle, and I sank back down onto my chair.

"Stephanie." My mom's voice was soft. She touched my hand.

"I did not run away! I did not make this up. Someone kidnapped me."

"Okay," Gregg said, his voice as soft as my mom's. He held up his hands in a gesture of surrender. "I didn't mean to upset you. I know you don't like me all that much, Steph, but I care about you. I care about you and your mom both. I was just asking, that's all."

My mom's hand was warm and soft on mine.

"Everything's okay, Stephanie. We believe you. *I* believe you." She glanced at Gregg. "Eat your supper, honey," she said to me.

I sat down, but only because it was important to my mom.

"I'm sorry," Gregg said again. "I should learn to keep my big mouth shut. I know it. I'm sorry."

After we finished eating, Gregg volunteered to clean up. My mom and I sat together on the couch in the family room. Gregg brought Mom a cup of tea. He offered me one too, but I told him no, thanks. By the time Gregg had put everything in the dishwasher and wiped down the counters, my mom was falling asleep beside me. Gregg knelt down in front of her and said, "You should go to bed, Trish."

My mom said no. "I want to be with my baby."

"Your baby is safe and sound," Gregg said. "See? She's right here. Nothing bad is going to happen to her, right, Steph?" I nodded. "And you haven't slept a wink all week. Come on. Up we go."

My mom wrapped her arms around his neck, and he helped her get up. He slipped an arm around her waist. As I watched them, I understood for the first time what my mom saw in him. Okay, so he wasn't my dad. But he wasn't that bad. And he sure seemed to care about her.

"I'm going to stay down here for a while and watch TV," I said.

Neither of them argued with me.

The house was quiet by the time I finally shut off the TV and climbed the stairs to my room. When I went into the bathroom to brush my teeth, there were clothes all over the floor—Gregg's clothes. Including—yuck!—his underwear. Instantly I felt the same old revulsion that I'd had for him before. My dad never left his clothes lying all over the floor for other people to pick up. But Gregg was like a spoiled teenager, and my mom never seemed to mind. Well, I wasn't going to pick up his disgusting clothes. I hadn't changed that much. Instead I kicked them aside.

Then I remembered how I had felt when I was out there alone in the woods. I remembered how overjoyed I had been when my mom had finally been allowed to see me at the police station—and how sensitive Gregg had been to me and how attentive he'd been to my mom. She must have gone through hell the whole time I was missing, and Gregg was the one who had been with her the whole time, looking after her, comforting her. I bent down and gingerly picked up his jeans and underwear—I wished I had rubber gloves on—and put them in the hamper.

Then I picked up his socks—they were white but the soles were black, as if he'd been walking around in his sock feet outside—and his shirt. I dumped them in the hamper too. I was closing the hamper lid when I noticed a mark—a sweat stain?—on the inside of the shirt collar. I picked up the shirt again and looked at it. I touched the mark. What *was* that? Something disgusting, no doubt.

Sunlight was streaming into my room when I opened my eyes the next morning. I glanced at my clock radio. Wait a minute. It wasn't morning at all. It was afternoon.

I heard a shriek from outside.

I got out of bed and hopped over to the window. My mom and Gregg were outside in the driveway washing Gregg's truck. My mom's T-shirt was soaked through. Gregg must have turned the hose on her. That's what that shriek was all about. Now he was grinning at her breasts. I wanted to like him. I wanted to feel the same way about him as I had felt when I was lost and afraid. But he made it so hard.

I got dressed and went outside. Gregg and my mom were wrestling over the hose like a couple of kids. My mom got the hose away from him and sprayed him the way he had sprayed her. He laughed and peeled off his T-shirt. Then he grabbed her and hugged her. She shrieked again. Mrs. Pendergast across the street looked at the two of them and shook her head. Maybe she did it because she was old and disapproved of everything. But I like to think she did it because she thought Gregg was as juvenile as I did. I turned to go back inside. That's when I got a good look at Gregg from behind. I stopped and stared at him.

"Stephanie," Mom said, finally noticing me. She looked refreshed and happy. "We thought you were going to sleep around the clock."

I thought about the night I had been taken. I thought about where everyone was.

"Stephanie?"

I jumped when someone touched my shoulder. It was my mom.

"Are you okay?" she said.

I nodded.

"Are you hungry? Do you want me to make you something to eat?"

"I'm good, Mom. I—I think I'm going to take a bath."

"You took such a long shower last night that we ran out of hot water," Gregg said.

"If we have to run out of hot water everyday for the rest of our lives because Stephanie wants to take long showers, that's okay with me," my mom said. She gave me a huge bear hug.

"Mom! You're soaking wet!"

"And you're going to be soaking wet in a few minutes too." She pointed the hose at me. I yelped and hobbled inside. I went straight upstairs to the bathroom. I tore the lid off the laundry hamper. It was empty.

The shirt was gone.

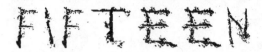

FIFTEEN

I made my way down to the basement. It was a lot harder going downstairs on crutches than it was going up. My mom must have done the laundry first thing in the morning. Both the washing machine and the dryer were empty, and the laundry basket was heaped with clean and carefully folded clothes. I pawed through it until I found Gregg's shirt. I opened it and looked at the collar. It was as clean as new. There was no trace of the mark I had seen the night before.

I was trying to decide what to do when I heard footsteps on the basement stairs. I threw the shirt onto the top of the hamper just as Gregg appeared. He looked surprised to see me.

"What are you doing down here, Steph?" he said. "I thought you were taking a bath."

"I…I came down to get some clean clothes."

His eyes went to the hamper. Was it just my imagination or was he wondering why his shirt wasn't neatly folded like everything else?

"You should have tons of clean clothes in your room," he said. "Did you look?"

I shook my head.

"I did the laundry a couple of days after you disappeared," he said.

"*You* did the laundry?" Gregg never did the laundry. He always dumped his stuff in the bathroom hamper and left it to Mom, who sometimes left it to me. I nearly gagged every time I had to touch a pair of his underwear.

"I know how to do laundry," he said. "I've been on my own for a long time. Besides, your mom was a real mess. Someone had to take things in hand."

He didn't expect me to believe *that*, did he? I had a pretty good idea why he had decided, for the first time ever, to take charge of washing the clothes. I hobbled past him and hurried upstairs. My mom was in the kitchen.

"I'm going over to Allison's," I said.

"Oh," my mom said. "I forgot to tell you. Allison called this morning. She wanted to know how you were."

"She was probably worried. That's why I want to see her."

"She *was* worried. But I told her you're all mine today. After what happened, I'm not letting you out of my sight. I want us to spend what's left of the day together. You can see Allison tomorrow."

"But—"

"Allison is fine with it, Stephanie. She understands how I feel." She hugged me again. I had never gotten so many hugs in one day. "Remember when you and I used to spend a whole afternoon in the kitchen making a gourmet dinner for your dad?"

I did. Every now and then my mom would decide she wanted to do something special. We'd go through cookbooks and magazines looking for delicious dishes that we had never tried, and then we'd be in the kitchen all day, making appetizers, a main course and a fancy dessert. We'd set the table with a linen tablecloth and the best china and silver, and my mom would light candles. My dad would choose music—always something classical—and we would pretend we were royalty, dining on the best food while an orchestra played just for us.

"I thought it would be fun to do that today," my mom said. "Just like we used to."

"But Dad—" I bit my tongue when I saw the flash of pain in her eyes. It was the first time in a long time that I'd seen that look, and I realized that no matter what I had thought and no matter who she was with now, she did miss my dad. She really did.

"Those were the best times, Stephanie," my mom said in a quiet voice. "The very best."

I wanted to cry when she said that.

"Okay, Mom." If that's what she wanted, I would do it. Besides, being in the kitchen together, it would give me a chance to check something out.

Gregg came upstairs.

"You two need some help in here?" he said.

"No. We're fine. We just need you out of the kitchen so that we can get busy."

"Mind if I watch the ball game on TV?"

"Yes," I said at the exact same time as my mom said, "No."

"I thought we could put some music on," I said to my mom. "Like we always used to."

She smiled. "We'll be fine without it. Go ahead and watch the game, Gregg. It'll be nice for us to be here all together."

Gregg grabbed a beer out of the fridge, took his run book off the desk in the corner of the kitchen and went into the family room to turn on the TV. He was there all afternoon, drinking beer and watching TV.

My mom and I cooked for the rest of the afternoon. I would have had a great time—if things had been different. But they weren't.

Gregg liked the food okay, but he wasn't crazy about the classical music. He switched to a rock station instead. My mom let him. She asked him to open a bottle of wine, but he wouldn't drink any of it.

"I'm a beer guy," he said. He sure was. And he didn't even bother with a glass. By the time supper was over, there were three empty beer cans on the table with the good china, my mom's best silver and a white linen tablecloth. I couldn't believe that I had ever thought I would be glad to be home as long as he was there.

Gregg volunteered to help me clean up the kitchen—he said my mom deserved to put her feet up after such a great meal—but he was too rough with my mom's china, so she told him, never mind, she'd do it instead. He insisted that he didn't want her to have to do anything, so I ended up helping him. He cleared the table and handed me the dishes, and I put them in the dishwasher. I must have looked at that newspaper article on the fridge a couple of dozen times as I worked—the one with the picture of those two girls and all the details about their disappearances, including the dates. As soon as we'd finished with the cleanup, I excused myself and went up to my room.

I lay on my bed in the dark, waiting. It took forever before I heard my mom's bedroom door click shut. I waited some more. I wanted to be sure they were both asleep. Then I eased my way downstairs to the kitchen. In the glow of a streetlight, I saw Gregg's run book. It was back on the desk near the phone. I grabbed it, carried it to the window and opened it to the date when the first girl had disappeared. Just as I had suspected—Gregg had been on a run that day. He'd been gone for two days. My fingers trembled as I flipped to the date the second girl had disappeared. Gregg had been on a run then too.

The kitchen suddenly flooded with light. I turned, hiding the run book behind my back.

"Hey, Steph," Gregg said, surprised. "What are you doing down here?"

"I—I was hungry."

"After that meal?" He was staring at me. I leaned back and put the run book back on the desk.

"What are you doing?" I asked.

"Your mom wanted some cold water."

"Can you pour me some too?"

He frowned at me but finally turned to the fridge. I quickly checked to make sure that the run book was exactly where he had left it. Then I went to him and took the glass of water from him. My hand shook as I drank it down.

"Thanks," I said.

I headed for the stairs.

"Hey, Steph," Gregg said. "I thought you said you were hungry."

I didn't know what to say, so I didn't say anything at all. I went back to my room and closed the door. I wished I could lock it, but I couldn't. I sat on the edge of my bed in the dark, waiting. It seemed like forever before I heard Gregg come back up the stairs and go into my mom's room. I waited some more. I waited forever. I wished I had a cell phone or a phone in my room, but I didn't. And I was afraid to go back downstairs again until I was sure Gregg was asleep. Even then, my heart was in my throat as I made my way back down the stairs on my crutches, clutching the card that Sergeant Andruksen had given me.

SIXTEEN

The doorbell rang first thing in the morning. Gregg answered it. I heard a familiar voice. It was Sergeant Andruksen.

"Good morning, Mr. Hamilton," he said. I hobbled to the door on my crutches and stood beside Gregg. Sergeant Andruksen nodded at me. Detective Carlysle was with him and there were two uniformed police officers on the porch. "We need to ask you a couple of questions."

"Me?" Gregg looked confused.

My mom came out of the kitchen to see who was at the door.

"Sergeant," she said. "Come in. Do you have any news for us? Did you catch the man who took Stephanie?"

Sergeant Andruksen and Detective Carlysle stepped inside.

"We'd like to see the back of your neck, Mr. Hamilton," Sergeant Andruksen said to Gregg.

"The back of his neck?" My mom looked completely lost. "I don't understand. What does Gregg's accident have to do with this?"

"It's okay. Let me handle this, Trish," Gregg said. "Why don't you go and put on a fresh pot of coffee?"

"What accident?" Sergeant Andruksen said.

"Gregg had an accident at work last week," my mom said.

"I said I'd handle this, Trish," Gregg said. His face was red, and he spoke through clenched teeth.

"What kind of accident?" Sergeant Andruksen said, asking the question that had just flashed in my mind. Had I made a huge mistake?

"It was nothing really," Gregg said. "It was stupid."

"Was it a car accident?" Detective Andruksen said.

"No. It happened at work," my mom said.

"Trish, please!" Gregg looked like he wished she was anywhere but in the hall with him.

"It's nothing to be embarrassed about," she said. "I gave Gregg a medallion on a chain. It was supposed to be for good luck, but it sure didn't bring any." The two cops frowned, and I bet they were wondering the same thing that I was—what did she mean? "Right after I gave him the medallion, everything seemed to go wrong after that. Two days later Stephanie vanished. Then—and I know this doesn't even begin to compare with what happened to Stephanie—but the chain got caught on a machine when Gregg was at work. He was alone when it happened. There was no one to help him. He was lucky he was able to stop that machine. Otherwise he would have been seriously hurt. As it was, the chain cut into his neck before it finally broke."

"May we see your neck?" Sergeant Andruksen asked Gregg.

"It's no big deal," Gregg said.

"I'd like to see it," Sergeant Andruksen said. It sounded like an order, not a request.

Gregg turned reluctantly and tugged down the neck of the sweater he was wearing. Sergeant Andruksen and Detective Carlysle both looked.

"When exactly did this happen?"

"The Monday after Stephanie disappeared," my mom said. "Isn't that right, Greg?"

Gregg nodded.

"It looks like it must have hurt," Sergeant Andruksen said. "Mrs. Rawls is right. That chain really cut into your neck. What happened to it? Where is it now?"

"It fell down a drain at work," my mom said. "Isn't that what you told me, Gregg?"

"Yeah."

"But he still has the medallion," my mom said. "He managed to catch it before it fell into the drain too." She reached out and squeezed Gregg's hand. Sergeant Andruksen and Detective Carlysle exchanged glances.

"That was quick thinking, under the circumstances," Sergeant Andruksen said.

"I guess that's the only luck we had," my mom said. "Until Stephanie came home again." Her eyes teared up. "I was going to buy Gregg a new chain, but, well, you know, I had more important things on my mind." She sniffled.

Sergeant Andruksen reached into his pocket and pulled out a photograph. He held it out to Gregg. It was a picture of the chain I had found.

"Did your chain look anything like this?" he asked.

Gregg looked at the photo. He shook his head. "I'm not sure. It was a just a regular chain," he said.

Sergeant Andruksen showed the picture to my mom. She seemed surprised to see it, but she studied it carefully before answering.

"That looks like the same kind of chain I bought Gregg," she said. "Why?"

"Stephanie says she pulled a chain—this chain—off her attacker," Sergeant Andruksen said. "It's a fairly sturdy chain, but as you can see, it's broken. If Stephanie pulled hard enough to break it, then it must have left quite a mark on the neck of whoever was wearing it."

My mom's eyes widened.

"Surely you don't think that Gregg had anything to do with what happened to Stephanie," she said.

Sergeant Andruksen looked at Gregg.

"Would you be willing to volunteer a DNA sample, Mr. Hamilton?" he said.

"A DNA sample? What for?" Gregg said.

"To eliminate you as a suspect."

"Suspect?" Gregg looked furious. "You think *I* kidnapped Stephanie? I'm about to marry her mom.

154

She's going to be my stepdaughter. No, I would not be willing to volunteer a DNA sample. How dare you accuse me!" He put an arm around my mom. "That's it," he said. "Please leave this house."

"I'm afraid we can't do that," Sergeant Andruksen said calmly. He produced a document from his jacket pocket. "We have a search warrant."

"Search warrant? What for?"

"To search this house and your apartment." He nodded to the two police officers on the porch. They stepped inside. "Where is your run book, Mr. Hamilton?"

"My run book?"

"It's on the desk in the kitchen," I said. Gregg gave me a sharp look.

My mom was staring at me. She seemed to have no idea what was going on. One of the police officers disappeared into the kitchen.

"We're also going to need the clothes you were wearing last Saturday—and the footwear. You can either give it to us or we can seize everything."

"This is crazy," my mom said.

"Mr. Hamilton?"

"I was wearing jeans and a sweatshirt," Gregg said. "But they've been washed."

"What about a jacket?" Sergeant Andruksen said. "And shoes?"

"I had on a brown leather jacket," Gregg said. "It's in the closet. So are my boots."

"Show the officer."

Gregg pointed them out for the second cop. The first one returned with the run book and handed it to Sergeant Andruksen, who flipped through it and then passed it to Detective Carlysle. He looked through it too.

"We need to ask you some more questions, Mr. Hamilton," he said. "You too, Mrs. Rawls. We'd like you to come with us."

My mom looked startled.

"What for? I don't understand."

"Are you arresting us?" Gregg demanded. "Because we don't have to go with you unless you arrest us."

"You're not under arrest," Sergeant Andruksen said. "But you want to help us figure out exactly what happened to Stephanie, don't you?"

"Of course we do," my mom said. "But—"

A cell phone trilled. Sergeant Andruksen pulled a phone out of his pocket and stepped aside to answer it. I heard him mention a name: Zeke. When he had finished the call, he waved Detective

Carlysle over. They spoke quietly together. Then Sergeant Andruksen said, "You can either come with us now, Mr. Hamilton, or we can wait here until I can get someone to bring over an arrest warrant."

"An arrest warrant?" my mom said. "For what? Gregg hasn't done anything."

"Mr. Hamilton?" Sergeant Andruksen said.

Gregg looked at the door and then at the two uniformed cops. He didn't say anything.

SEVENTEEN

The police handcuffed Gregg, and the two uniformed police officers took him to the police station in the back of a squad car. My mom and I rode with Sergeant Andruksen and Detective Carlysle. When we got there, Detective Carlysle took Gregg into one interview room, and Sergeant Andruksen went with my mom into another one. I waited in the outer office. While Sergeant Andruksen talked to mom, another police officer called him out of the room and talked to him. The same police officer knocked on the door of the other interview room and said something to Detective Carlysle. Finally Sergeant Andruksen came and sat down beside me.

"Where's my mom?" I said.

"She's making a formal statement."

"A formal statement? She didn't do anything, did she?"

"No. But we need to record what she knows about the accident and about Gregg's whereabouts the day you disappeared."

"It was him, wasn't it?" I felt kind of shaky when I thought about him. He had been practically living at my house. He had been going to marry my mom. "He's the serial killer."

"He's the person who drugged you and left you in that shack, Stephanie. He admitted it. He didn't have much choice."

"What do you mean?"

"We found trace amounts of blood on that chain. They match Gregg's blood type. We also found trace amounts of blood on the collar of his jacket. When we do a DNA analysis, we'll be able to confirm that it's his blood on that chain."

I had figured out as much when I saw the mark on his neck.

"What about that mark on his shirt? Did he tell you about that?" I asked.

"It was makeup."

"Makeup?"

"When he came to the police station that time, knowing you were alive, he covered the mark on his neck, just in case. I guess he didn't want to have to answer any awkward questions. We also have a link between him and that shack you were in."

"You *found* the shack?"

"Zeke did. He backtracked you. He found a shack that matches the description you gave me, and he found the rope that was used to tie you up. It turns out the shack belonged to an uncle of an old friend of Gregg's. The place has been abandoned for fifteen years or so. Gregg's friend hasn't been to it since his uncle died. He was surprised to hear that the place was still standing. But Gregg knew. And you were right about the night you were taken. Gregg had a run booked up around Birch Lake. He was supposed to drive up there and back."

"And he didn't make the trip?"

"He made it. But he showed up about six hours later than he was supposed to. He told the manager at one of the machine locations that he had some kind of family emergency." Sergeant Andruksen paused to let everything sink in. "We also found a gas-station operator near Ogden who remembered that Gregg had stopped there for gas late Saturday night."

"Ogden?" I said. "That's nowhere near Birch Lake."

"No, it isn't, which accounts for some of the lost time," Sergeant Andruksen said. "Birch Lake isn't far from Angel Falls, and it's even closer to that shack. We decided to check if anyone had seen him in the vicinity of the cabin, and we found the gas-station operator. We also talked to the manager of the store where your mother says she bought the medallion and chain for Gregg. He had a copy of the receipt, and he was able to identify the chain as identical to the one he sold your mother."

I was still having trouble believing it.

"Gregg is a serial killer."

Sergeant Andruksen was silent for a moment.

"About the other two girls who were taken," he said finally. "Both of them were buried in shallow graves, which means that they didn't escape like you did. Somebody buried them—most likely the same person who murdered them. They'd been chained, not tied with a rope. And we found no evidence that they'd been drugged."

At first I didn't understand what he was telling me. What difference did it make that Gregg had used chains on the other two girls and a rope on me?

What difference did it make that they hadn't been drugged? Then I remembered what Derek Fowler had told everyone in school: serials killers are all about patterns and rituals. Sergeant Andruksen was telling me that what had happened to me didn't fit the same pattern as what had happened to those other two girls.

"You don't think Gregg took those girls, do you?" I said.

"We're pretty sure he didn't. The DNA sample will confirm it for us. But he was afraid that's exactly what we thought, especially with all the evidence we had that he'd been lying to us. That's why he confessed."

I started to shake as I thought about what that meant.

"It was me," I said. "He just wanted to kill me."

"He took advantage of the disappearances of those other two girls," Sergeant Andruksen said softly. "He was well aware of the similarities between you and them in terms of age and appearance. He used that to make it seem that you were the third victim. He drugged you, tied you up and left you in that shack, where he was pretty sure no one would find you—until it was too late. He said he planned to go back there eventually and..." He didn't finish his sentence. He didn't have to. I remembered how those other two girls had been found.

"But why?" I said. "Why would he do that to me?"

"He said he did it because he loved your mother."

"He did it for *her*?"

Sergeant Andruksen shook his head. "He did it because when he met your mother, it was just the two of them. You were up north with your grandfather. He said everything was different when you came back. He wanted her for himself. He said they had plans together."

They were going to start a business. They were going to use the money my dad had left.

"He also said that every time you and your mother got into an argument, your mother would say they'd have to wait. She told him she didn't want you any more upset than you already were after what happened to your father, and to give you time, that you would change your mind about him once you got to know him better. Gregg was tired of waiting."

I wasn't sure I wanted to ask the next question, but I had to know.

"And my mom?"

"What about her?"

"Did she know?"

"He says she didn't."

He says.

"Do you believe him?"

"We have no evidence to suggest otherwise."

No evidence? What did that mean?

"Did she know or not?" I said.

"We've talked to the chief of police here, and to her friends. She seemed genuinely distraught over your disappearance, Stephanie. We have no reason to doubt that her emotions were real."

I wanted more than that. I wanted a definite no: No, your mother didn't know anything about it. We're one hundred percent positive.

My mom came out of the interview room. Her reddened eyes and puffy face told me that she had been crying. She asked if she could see Gregg.

"I'm afraid not," Sergeant Andruksen said. "I'll get someone to take you and Stephanie home."

My mom was so upset. She kept saying she couldn't believe what was happening. She said she'd thought she'd known him so well. She'd been going to marry him. He'd even talked about starting a new family.

"How could I have been so wrong?" she said. She said it over and over again for a long time. It really shook her up that she hadn't even begun to guess what was going on. She said it so often and looked so upset every time that I was finally convinced that she'd had no idea what Gregg was up to. I heard her tell one of her friends she was never going to get married again. She wasn't even sure she wanted to date. "How can I trust my judgment?" she said.

Gregg went to prison.

But the cops didn't find the serial killer. As far as I know, he's still out there. I never take short-cuts anymore. I don't even like to walk alone. And if I have to be somewhere after dark, I always call my mom, and she always comes to get me.

NORAH McCLINTOCK is a five-time winner of the Crime Writers of Canada's Arthur Ellis Award for Best Juvenile Crime Novel. Although Norah is a free-lance editor, she still manages to write at least one novel a year. She lives with her family in Toronto, Ontario, Canada.